BARB

BROKEN TRUTH NO MORE

A NOVEL

TATE PUBLISHING & *Enterprises*

Published by Tate Publishing & Enterprises, LLC
127 E. Trade Center Terrace | Mustang, Oklahoma 73064 USA
1.888.361.9473 | www.tatepublishing.com

Tate Publishing is committed to excellence in the publishing industry. The company reflects the philosophy established by the founders, based on Psalm 68:11,
"The Lord gave the word and great was the company of those who published it."

Cover design by Rebekah Garibay
Interior design by Joel Uber

Published in the United States of America

ISBN: 978-1-61739-336-5
1. Fiction, Christian, Futuristic
2. Fiction, Christian, Suspense
10.10.11

To my God, who makes all things possible.
To my family, who are the greatest encouragers in the world, especially Will.
To my country, which offers unlimited opportunities.

What if you slept?

And what if in your sleep, you dreamed?

And what if in your dream, you went to heaven and there plucked a strange and beautiful flower?

And what if, when you woke, you had the flower in your hand?

Ah! What then?

—Samuel Taylor Coleridge

CHAPTER I

It was fall. The trees had changed to the colors of the season: red, orange, yellow, and brown. They were quite spectacular. In another world the area would have been prime resort real estate. Nature lovers would have flocked to the area to behold the beauty of the place. Tall mountains, rippling streams, and colorful wildflowers dotted the terrain. The small village would have been a place of peace and rest. Instead, the community was a place to exist in a hostile world. The beauty of the surroundings, however, was not lost to the occupants of the village. They appreciated nature's gifts and managed to survive with her help. It was colder earlier this year. The cold was much sharper because there was no heat. Heat sources had to be saved for the really severe cold. Life was hard. This was just one of many inconveniences. Truly amazing. Man could survive with so little. Mind you, survive, not thrive.

Life had long ago taken a turn toward survival, but the old man Paul Allen would not give up. Perhaps it was the memories. Perhaps it was in his DNA. Whatever it was, he and his cohorts were determined man would once again thrive. They not only had hope; they had a plan. Dangerous though it was, the plan would work. It had to. They would have only one chance. If they failed… well, he tried never to think of failure.

The plan was conceived long ago. At first, it was like a trickle of sunlight filtering through dark storm clouds. As time went on, the sky became clearer and clearer. Yes, it would work. After all, it was a plan imagined at a time of failure. All wrong ways were clearly posted. It had captivated him. It held his attention. He never forgot.

The old man sat in the hard chair. So long ago, the aged man would have had a soft cushion for comfort. Now only a strong, wooden chair with rickety arms supported his seventy-five-year-old frame. He knew it was almost time for his grandson to return. He carefully unfolded a blanket and spread it across his lap. He had time for a quick nap before Nat would come bursting through the door, but he decided against slumber. The dreams would come—some good, some not so good. He took no chances. Somehow, they always made the present seem so bleak. If the memories ran through his mind while he was fully conscious, they were like a refreshing spring day, not as vivid as the dreams, but just as soothing.

For reasons known only to the man and the group, Paul Allen feigned to be feeble. Actually, he was as strong as a team of mules. No one outside the group, not even his daughter, knew the truth. Paul knew that someday questions could be asked and convincing truthfulness would be important. His daughter, Marsha, had never been good at lying, and he wasn't about to put her on the spot at this late date.

In spite of himself, the old man fell into a slumber. The dreams came, and he remembered. The good dreams, and he remembered. So vivid, so clear, so wonderful, and he remembered. The farm flashed into his mind. Rolling green pastures, it was a young boy's heaven on earth. Off in the distance, he saw Pops. Pops was bush hogging. Pops could make short order of those fields with that bright green tractor. Pops was far away, but a skip and a hop and he would be in G's kitchen. His earliest memories were the smell of chocolate chip bars cooling in his grandmother's kitchen. G was the best cook alive, except maybe his mom. The door slammed, and Paul was drawn reluctantly out of his sleep.

Unknown to Paul, his grandson, Nat, had been watching him sleep. The ten-year-old grew impatient and slammed the door to get the old man's attention. It worked. Nat observed the man sleeping and couldn't help but ask if he had been having the good dreams. The man acknowledged that they were indeed the best of dreams. Nat knew the answer without even asking. The good dreams always brought a smile across the old man's face while he was sleeping. Nat had heard the stories—the good stories that is. He had also been present when the not so good dreams came. Tears would stream down Gramps's face, and the old man would scream. It always terrified Nat, and he was very slow to ask questions about those dreams. However, Gramps always reassured him that everything was fine. Nat never pressed his grandfather about the bad dreams.

He hoped he would never have to hear the abominable stories associated with those dreams.

The best Nat could tell, Gramps's life was a before and after picture. The stories Gramps told were beyond his wildest imagination. Nat sometimes felt that Gramps was just a great storyteller, but there was always a ring of truth to what he said. Gramps would always assure him that he was speaking the truth. All stories came with the warning "you must never, and I mean never, tell these stories to anyone."

Nat could not help wondering about the food and clothes, but what really gave him pause was all the talk about things he had only seen in books, the things Gramps called the finer things in life. This was so different from what they called them in the outside world. Evil. That's what they were called in the book he had unknowingly run across one day at his school. In the hands of the masses, luxuries were evil, but it always seemed strange to him that the elites had all of these things. This, according to the book, was good.

Nat knew that Gramps was no elite, but Gramps told stories of having things as a child that many elites did not have. He described huge homes, vacations, even church on Sunday. Nat could imagine no such existence. How did one attain that level? No wonder the stories were secret. Nat cringed at what could happen to him and Gramps for just thinking such foolishness. Surely Gramps was exaggerating, but what if he wasn't?

Nat was the only person to whom the old man told the stories though Paul was sure Marsha overheard the storytelling. Paul knew better than to endanger the chance of success, but he was confident that Marsha would never say a word. It was risky to tell Nat, but there was no other way to prepare him for the quickly approaching moment when Nat might have to decide on matters far beyond his ten years of life. If he made the wrong choices, and he hoped no such decisions would have to be made, Paul knew he would believe his whole life had been lived in vain. Then the stories would be all he had. No hope, just stories.

"Gramps, tell me a story."

"Which one, or would you prefer a new one?"

Nat thought for a moment and finally said, "Tell me about the Beast."

Paul smiled. Nat always loved hearing about his pet from long ago. Perhaps it was because Nat would never own a dog. The state deemed pets a frivolous distraction. The animal was affectionately known as the Beast. The Irish setter earned that name from destroying anything within her sight. As she grew older, she had settled a little, but was still very much a handful.

The man carefully began his story: "On a beautiful, spring day as the earth was awakening from a particularly long, hard, cold winter, I decided the time had come to tame the Beast. With leash in hand, I approached the beautiful, blonde dog. The dog would do anything for me, or so I thought. However, she was unsure about being attached to a long cord. As fate would have it, just as I attached the cord to her collar, Itty Bitty the cat jumped in front of the Beast. No amount of hollering was going to stop her. The problem was I was attached to the other end of the cord. Bright idea, huh? I ran with all my might to keep up with her frantic pace, but I was wearing down. She, on the other hand, had caught a second wind. Through the fields she ran with me in tow always two dog lengths behind the cat. The pond was approaching, and she was going faster and faster. I screamed for the Beast to stop to no avail. Finally, there we were at the pond's edge going full steam. The Beast tore right through the water dragging me along trying to take a short cut to head off the cat, which wisely stayed on the bank. I was eating mud and drinking stale water so fast I thought I would drown. Up the bank of the pond we ran. Finally, she stopped. No more running. In fact, she froze. As I looked down, the biggest rattlesnake I had ever seen crossed our path. I didn't dare move as the snake slinked away from us. The Beast looked at me as if to express great sorrow for having put me in harm's way. All was forgiven until I led her back to the house, and Mom took a look at us. But that's a story for another day."

"Gramps, you reckon I could have a dog?"

"Son, I don't see how. Even if we could slip one in, they make a lot of noise, not to mention they eat a lot of food. Food costs a lot of money."

"You had money. Why don't I?"

"Nat, it was a different time, a different world."

Then the boy said what the old man had been waiting to hear, "I want to be a part of the world you grew up in."

"Would you really?"

Then the boy said something that caught the old man completely off guard. "Free. Gramps, that's what I want. I want to be free."

Tears streamed down the man's face and dropped to the plank floor. "Someday. Someday, Nat, I will make sure you have the opportunity to be free. But for now, we exist. *Free*, what a beautiful word. What a wonderful word indeed."

CHAPTER 2

The boy scampered into another room as his mother called him. It was time for the state-sanctioned rituals. Even though Marsha did not agree with the ceremony, she knew it was in Nat's best interests to go along with the charade. Nat had been told early on that he should participate but to always remember that it was the inside that counted. Nat understood the concept because he had given his heart to Jesus a few years earlier. The boy believed this exercise to be one that only wasted time. Time he would have rather been spending with Gramps. But the state wanted control, and they thought a few repetitions would give them the power. The elites were so involved grabbing power that they didn't realize that a force was growing in the country. They were occupied with their "wisdom." Bad mistake.

The old man had no intention of waiting for the unrest to amplify. With the restlessness would ultimately come

chaos. Nat had to be protected. His generation was the future, a future like Paul's past. That's what he wanted for the boy, and the plan would ensure that future.

Remember. Paul needed to remember. The thoughts would somehow give him the confidence he would need in the days ahead. The good, the bad, and everything in between had to be remembered. The old man closed his eyes, and he remembered. He wanted to go back, back as far as he could touch memories, back to a different time and place, back to a different world…

Paul was six years old. He smelled the honeysuckle in the fencerow. He didn't know why, but honeysuckle always gave off such a sweet fragrance that he instantly sneezed. He didn't mind. That smell meant spring, and he loved it. This was his and Pops's day. Pops had promised a day at the lake with nothing but fishing. Paul was determined to catch that big ol' catfish that always seemed to make fun of him as he swished under the dock. He and Pops jumped in the truck and headed for the lake house. The rest of the family would be coming down late in the afternoon, and it was the responsibility of the "menfolk" to catch supper.

"Pops, you reckon I might catch ol' Blubber today?"

"Sure hope you do. That fish will feed the whole bunch. You never know. Fish will sometimes bite, and sometimes they don't. You take what you get, and you don't pitch a fit."

Upon arriving, he and Pops went into the house. The house had been closed for a while, and the odor from being shut up was apparent. Paul knew the smell would be gone in short order. Spring had come, and someone would be at the house almost every week. “Can we go down to the dock?” Paul asked Pops. “I’m ready to catch Blubber.”

“Okay, okay. Give me just a minute to get a little organized. You know the others are not going to like it if they get here and the house is not good and cool.” The heat had been left on all winter, and it was time to click the switch.

Finally, Pops and Paul made their way down the railroad-tie steps to their private dock. Life was good, and the boy knew this was how life was supposed to be. He didn’t know it then, but he was an advantaged child. Furthermore, he didn’t understand the mechanics of how much hard work had been performed to reach this pinnacle. Pops occasionally told him stories, and he loved them; however, he had not reached the point in the maturing process to be able to translate the stories into dollars and cents. All he knew was that Blubber was there waiting to be caught.

Pops baited Paul’s hook and then his own. Even at six, Paul was quite proficient at casting, though baiting was something that still made him cringe. He was a kind-hearted child and was sure that he was hurting the bait. On the other hand, he was just as sure Pops made those creatures like what they were experiencing.

At long last, Paul cast his line right where he thought ol’ Blubber would be. He got a few nibbles and soon discovered his bait was missing. Once again, Pops fixed his bait on the hook. Pops always knew the fishing trips were for the boy, so he simply planned on casting between helping Paul. Life was good, and Pops knew it too.

Paul managed to land a few small fish, and so did Pops. Between them, they had enough for supper. Still Paul was not satisfied. "Pops, can we try just one more time. I really want to catch Blubber."

"One more time. That's all. We've got to dress these fish and get ready for the rest of the family to eat."

"Thanks, Pops. I just know he's going to jump on this line and beg to be eaten."

Pops smiled and thought, *Yeah right.*

Pops skepticism soon faded when, just as Paul cast the line, it took off. "Help me, Pops. I can't hold it."

"Yes, you can. Let him run just a little and then start reeling him in."

Paul did just as Pops instructed, and in came the biggest catfish Paul had ever seen. As Pops netted him, he noticed tears running down Paul's cheeks. "What's the matter, Son?"

"He wasn't supposed to be caught."

Pops said, "Someone had to catch him eventually. It might as well be you."

"We can't keep him," Paul announced.

"What?"

"We've got enough for supper. We can't keep Blubber. Please, Pops, let's throw him back."

"Okay, if you're absolutely sure, but first, let's get a picture of you next to Blubber. The others might doubt us if we don't have proof."

"Sure, but hurry. He needs to get back in the lake. Blubber was born for open water. He's a fish leader." Paul looked one last time at the enormous fish before releasing him. Even at the tender age of six, he realized freedom came at a price. Blubber had almost lost his freedom and his life. Paul hoped the fish would be smarter next time. Never again did Paul see Blubber. He had hopefully learned his lesson…

As the old man opened his eyes, he thought to himself, *If I ever get my freedom again, I'll be smarter too.*

Nat had finished his rituals and was back in the room. He knew the old man was remembering. For some reason, he didn't want to know the story. Maybe it was the peacefulness coupled with urgency on Gramps's face. Whatever it was, he didn't ask.

"Nat, you remember that fish picture I showed you a while back."

"Sure do. How could I forget it! What a fish! You were only six, weren't you?"

"If I can talk your mom into it, reckon we could go fishing for a few days? Just the two of us."

"Wow!" Then a somber look came on the boy's face. "We'd have to get permission from one of the elites."

"I think I can make one of them see reason. How about it?"

"Sure! Just name the day and time."

"Oh, I'll let you know. Maybe ol' Blubber is still out there or at least his spirit."

The plan was being placed in motion. There was no turning back. Paul loved his grandson so much. He had to be offered a better life. How he hoped he would be able to give him freedom. Paul started playing "what if" mind games and quickly realized they were not useful. Nat would have the opportunity to experience a free life if he had to move heaven and earth. That much he knew.

CHAPTER 3

The time was drawing near. Paul sensed it. No matter how much propaganda was out there, truth always had a way of filtering through the lies. The unrest was growing. The old man had considered writing letters of good-bye to his daughter and then disappearing. If he took that course of action, it was time to write the two letters that he knew would break her heart. He had to believe that she would understand. Someday she might even thank him, but for now forgiveness and hope was what he wanted from Marsha. Marsha had a story too. She had felt her share of pain. It seemed everyone she loved was ripped out of her life; however, his actions would probably be the most cruel of all. Paul remembered Renee, Marsha's mother. A smile spread across Paul's face…

Renee was beautiful. Paul had first met Renee while they were in training school. They were being analyzed for the assignments that would best serve the common good. They dared not show any affection for each other. Affection was not good for the masses. No matter what the facilitators said, Paul knew Renee was the woman for him. Soon, they were slipping around meeting each other when and where they could. Finally, one day in early spring, Paul proposed to Renee; and of course, Renee with tears in her eyes had said, "Yes, forever and ever."

Permission had been granted by the state because their assignments had been similar. The state thought that a union of the two might produce superior offspring. The marriage had been a simple signing on the dotted line, no promises, no music, no guests. Simple signatures sufficed. Paul and Renee made their promises in private, and they meant their vows would be kept.

As best as could be expected, life for the couple had been kinder than for many. They were granted a small apartment with electricity and indoor plumbing. It was a far cry from what he remembered as a child, but it was so much better than what it could have been. They worked each day for the government, drew a small paycheck, and paid their bills. According to the official state elite, "What more could you possibly ask for?"

Freedom! That's what you could ask for, Paul thought but dared not express.

Renee shared Paul's dream for a better existence because she too had grown up "privileged." The elites always kept a close check on those couples in that situation. The smallest hint of unrest and one or the other could easily disappear, or at the least, they could lose their home. The only thing tolerated was conformity to the wishes of the state. Paul and Renee's dream would be their secret, their hope.

Only the grave itself would reveal their thoughts, and they knew the elites were not sharp enough to read minds.

After two years of marriage, Renee made a startling announcement to Paul. "I'm pregnant."

Paul's countenance changed. His usual smile turned to the most painful look Renee had ever witnessed from her thirty-five-year-old husband. "I know what you're thinking," she moaned. "I'm not very far along. Maybe we can fake dates. Perhaps permission will be granted for the pregnancy. If not, we'll leave, go somewhere. I really don't know, but I plan on having this baby."

The following day they filled out all the necessary paperwork without revealing the truth, and strangely, the following week they received permission to become pregnant. Renee had an easy pregnancy, and when Marsha was born two months premature, the midwife could not help but comment on how well developed the baby was to have arrived so early. She just smiled and left. There were still those who had a touch of humanity buried within themselves.

Marsha was immediately placed in a state-sponsored nursery because Renee had to return to work. Paul and Renee feigned sickness several days so that Marsha would not have to go. As time went on, Marsha developed into an independent youngster. Paul was delighted that she had such an "I'll do it on my own" spirit.

Marsha had just turned eight, and Renee discovered that she was once again pregnant. Paul knew this was not going to be acceptable to the state. The couple went to the reproductive clinic and were very shocked when they were assured that they would receive the necessary pregnancy permission; however, Renee would have to agree to one small test before the application could be processed. Without thinking, Paul and Renee agreed to the supposed test. Two days later, Renee miscarried.

Even as an old man, Paul still blamed himself for all the events that transpired. It was bad enough that they had been tricked into a state-sanctioned miscarriage that was really a delayed abortion, but infection ensued. Renee didn't get better. Three weeks after the miscarriage/abortion, Renee died.

From the moment of Renee's death, Paul's life was dedicated to Marsha. He dared not tell her the stories from his childhood. He was terrified of losing her. Paul always believed the state was watching, always ready to pounce, always ready to grab Marsha from his watchful care.

From the time of her mother's death, Marsha always had a sad look on her face. Paul did not like sending the child to the state-sponsored school, where she would be told he knew not what about the passing of her mother. He wanted to know what his daughter was being taught. He knew the lies he had been fed as a youngster and how his mom had patiently explained the truth. He feared he might fail Marsha.

Paul was a child of high intelligence and understood the meaning of "keep your truth to yourself." It eventually became a ritual that he would rush home, whenever he was allowed to go home, excited to tell his mother, Lenora, the things he had learned. She would then expound words of truth to him. The truth… that's what he wanted, the truth. The elites somehow made the masses believe a lie when the truth would have been much better for all. How was he going to make Marsha realize that the indoctrination sessions were designed to fill her with lies. She had to know the truth. She had to have an opportunity to know. To know? To know what? That was the question Paul grappled with for the next few months.

Finally, the answer was so clear. It amazed him that he had not realized sooner. How could such a simple concept have escaped him. Maybe it was his grief, maybe his fear of losing Marsha, or maybe a combination of the two. Either way, the process had clouded his thinking. It was so obvious. Truth brings freedom. The truth must be known before real freedom can take place. Marsha needed to be free. She must know the truth of the past. Only then could she be truly free.

CHAPTER 4

Days turned into weeks, weeks into months as Paul plotted his plan. Somehow he had to get Marsha away from the circumstances that would make her a cold, state-supported zombie. They must carefully make an exit from their present life. Paul and Marsha would start a new life. Paul formed new identities for the pair. He had access to some very important papers where he worked. Yes, this plan would work. Marsha would have the chance to decide some things for herself. After all, that's what freedom was all about.

Little did Paul know that he was being watched. A snitch had noticed that Paul was a little too preoccupied with the records department, and she did not hesitate to regurgitate all she observed. The state honored those with little ability and big noses.

On the day Paul was set to take Marsha and exit their old lives, a van pulled in front of the apartment

building. This was not unusual in and of itself, but when the men baled out of the van carrying guns, Paul knew. Just as he had known things in the past, he knew. Life was going to be different but not in the way he had planned. Fear gripped him. His worst nightmare was about to take place in front of his eyes. Just as things could get no more horrifying, the door burst open. Four thugs carrying huge weapons entered. "We're looking for Paul Allen," the largest man said.

Softly, he said, "That's me."

"We're here to take your daughter into state custody."

"Why? For what? I don't understand."

"The state has deemed you a threat to the well-being of the child. Where is she?"

At that moment, Marsha came out of the bedroom. Her curiosity quickly turned to fear. "Who are these people? What do they want?"

All Paul could utter was, "I'm sure there's a mistake."

The big man replied without even looking at the terrified pair, "No mistake. Here's the papers. Read them. Then sign them."

Paul was shaking as he accepted the notice. The document plainly said that Marsha was to be temporarily removed from the home. Paul was to appear in front of an elite in two weeks, when the matter would be resolved.

Paul knew there was no fighting this one, at least not now. "Marsha, you will have to go with these people for now. In a couple of weeks, we'll be back together."

Tears streamed down Marsha's cheeks. "I don't want to go. I want to stay with you. Please, don't let them take me. Ple-e-ease, Dad! Please!"

"Marsha, it will be okay."

Paul wanted to say much more, but before he could get the words out of his mouth, the animals disguised as people had grabbed Marsha and were out the door. To this day, Paul could still hear her cries as they rushed her out to the waiting van. Paul felt less than a human. How could he have let such a thing happen? Why hadn't he fought? The answer scared him. He feared that he too had become a part of the state. Submissive. Guilt riddled his shell of a body. Somehow, someway, Paul was going to get Marsha back. The next time he would be smarter. He would manage to stay a step ahead of these people. He would get another chance. In fact, his life would be built around a second chance, and it would not be wasted.

As soon as the van was out of sight, Paul grabbed his bike and headed for the Child Settlement Office. He had no idea what he would be told, but he had to fight for Marsha and fight hard. Upon arriving, he entered a building that smelled of mold. The lack of proper lighting made it difficult to find the rather small signs above the various doors. In its day, the building had probably been quite spectacular, but it had sagged to the expectations of its occupants. Finally, there it was: Child Settlement Office. Paul entered rather cautiously. He noticed a woman with her hair drawn back in a bun sitting at a desk to his right. Paul sheepishly asked, "May I speak with someone about a matter concerning my child?"

Without looking up, the receptionist said, "Of course. Take a number and find a place to stand over in the corner."

Paul could not help noticing how cold and matter-of-factly the woman spoke. She probably saw people like him every day, and now she was indifferent. Her humanity was all but gone. There was no spark. There was no zeal. She truly didn't care any more about his problem than the roach that was quickly approaching her desk. Smack! It was gone, and he knew that was what she planned to do with his problem. Still, he waited patiently. Minutes turned into hours. At last, the woman with the bun hairdo called him to her desk. "Now, what is your problem?" she coldly asked.

"My child, Marsha Allen, was taken from me by four men. They drove one of your vans. I'm here to retrieve her." Paul thought he sounded as cold as the bun lady.

"Sir, your hearing is in two weeks."

"I can't wait two weeks." Paul tried to remain calm.

"I don't know where she has been relocated."

"Relocated? I demand that she be relocated to the place from where she was removed."

"Sir, demands are frowned upon. Rules. We must go by rules—nothing more, nothing less."

Paul took a deep breath. "I'm sorry. Let me start over. I have a daughter who was kidnapped from our home. I respectfully request that she be returned."

"Sir, no matter how you say it, I still don't know where she is. You'll have to appear for your hearing in two weeks. Perhaps your caseworker will have knowledge of her whereabouts."

The bun lady's words were no more out of her mouth than she called the next number. Paul slowly left the room. He was numb. Two weeks was a long time to know nothing about where your child was, but his options were few. In an earlier life, Pops would have had the best private investigator on the case in less time than you could have blinked your eye. He would have stopped at nothing.

Police, national guard, whatever it took to get a family member back, that's what Pops would have done. If all else failed, he would have searched himself. That's how Pops was. That's why he was dead. Being dead was not what Paul needed. He needed clearness of mind. He needed to think. Paul left the dark, smelly building and headed back to the apartment.

The following morning Paul decided to keep busy. Two weeks would surely go faster if he stayed involved with other things. Worry was not going to help Marsha. Decisive action would have a better chance. As Paul approached his workplace, his entire life seemed very different. Somehow, he knew his entire being was changing forever. Call it intuition or something you grow to expect when living in a hostile society, but he felt strongly that his existence was about to change even more drastically.

Upon reaching the second floor, Paul turned left where his cubicle was at the far end. He didn't mind working at a cubicle. After all, most of his preparation was done at home in the apartment, where things were much quieter with fewer distractions. As he sat down in his chair that was beginning to show its age, he noticed an official-looking memo. It read:

> Please report to the main office on the first floor. Bring any personal belongings that you have in your work station. Anything which was supplied by the state, please leave behind.

Paul had few personal belongings that he would have left in the cubicle, so it was quite easy to gather everything into a neat, little bundle. But why should he take anything? What was happening? Paul made his way back down the steps to the first floor. He knew the main office was at the far end of the long hallway to the right. Upon entering the office, the secretary offered him a seat and in a very professional voice said, "Mr. Snell will be with you in a few minutes."

Paul did not know what was going on, but he suspected it couldn't be good. Across the room, a young man sat at a small corner desk. The young man occasionally looked in Paul's direction as if to say, "I need to talk to you." Neither of them made any effort at conversation. Perhaps it was because Paul had far more pressing things on his mind. Perhaps the young man sensed the time was not right. Either way, the encounter was like the two had an unfinished dialogue that would be taken up at a later time.

Finally, Mr. Snell summoned Paul to his office. "Paul, you've been a good employee, but I'm afraid I must terminate your employment. The state says you have become a risk. You know how they are when it comes to young, impressionable minds. I'm sorry. I wish you the best."

That's all there was to it. There was no good-bye party, no pats on the back. He received nothing but a handshake and a closed door on the way out.

Paul suspected, but now he knew. Marsha's removal and his job loss were all related. He tried to find a common denominator. He searched to find something that linked the two events. He thought and thought. Finally, he remembered the young woman who always seemed to conveniently be at the record room as he was making his plans for the future. She always seemed to ask too many questions about things that were none of her business. She had to have been the snitch. Paul became very angry.

By nature, Paul was an easy-going person, but enough was enough. He grabbed his bike and pedaled as hard and as fast as he could. The anger boiled, and he pedaled. By the time he started to calm, he had reached the outskirts of town. He slowly turned around and made his way to the lonely apartment. He immediately noticed a note on his door. It read:

> Please vacate this apartment by the end of the month.

He didn't even have to guess. He knew this was all part of crossing the state. This was to be a lesson not only to him but to all who dared cause ripples however small. Suddenly Paul was fearful, not for himself, but for his daughter, for her future, for her existence.

CHAPTER 5

The thoughts were too much for the old man. Paul had to have a break from the memories, but the relief only brought another stress: the letters. If he chose to write letters, what would he say? How would he say the truth with as little pain as possible? The letter the elites would be given was easy. It would be straightforward with no emotion, just facts. There would be no need to sugar-coat his whereabouts to the elites. Most of them were so incompetent it would never occur to them to check out the letter until it was far too late. After all, he was just an old man waiting out his time. Time that Paul realized was very crucial. He was already to the age if he had a medical problem, he would be denied treatment. He was useless in the eyes of the state. If he became sick and Marsha could not care for him, he would be sent to the Life Cycle Center. This was just a fancy name for state-sanctioned termination.

When the terminally ill and elderly went through that door, they never returned.

As a teenager, Paul and his best friend, Carney, had decided they would have some fun and sneak onto the grounds of the forbidden place. At the last moment, Paul's friend chickened out but not Paul. He climbed the fence and approached the tall, brown building. Paul saw a lit window and gravitated toward it. He would never forget what he saw. A gurney was next to a cold, sterile-looking table. An elderly man lay on the gurney. His wrinkled arms were strapped tight, almost to the point of cutting his blood flow. His aged ankles were cuffed so that he could not move. Tears rolled out of the corners of his eyes. "Please," he begged his supposed caregivers. "I feel so much better. If you'll call my daughter, I'm sure she'll come for me. Please." It was as if the walking corpses heard nothing. Instead, they injected the man. He struggled to no avail, and soon, he was gone.

Paul ran as fast as he could. He scaled the fence and never looked back. Carney asked him what he saw. He never answered, but he remembered. Now, he was an old man. He must change his fate, but more importantly, he must change the fate of Nat. The time had come. The memory made him a more determined man.

The memory gave him a reprieve from toying with the letter idea, but he had to decide if the letters would be the correct course of action. In his mind, Paul composed the first letter. It would simply read: "Nat and I received permission to go fishing. You know how slow moving I am these days. We will probably be gone for two or three days, maybe longer. Don't worry. We'll be fine. Dad."

The letter would be very short and straightforward. When the time came, Paul would place the notes on the table next to Marsha's bed. This note would be on top with instructions on the outside. The directions would say: "Read this first. Show this note to the elites if they question you. Read the bottom note last and destroy it." Paul wasn't at all sure that this was the thing to do, and he certainly had not composed the words for the last letter. The words would not come for his farewell letter to Marsha. He could not even come up with an opening sentence. All words seemed hollow to him. Maybe he couldn't begin the letter because it was the wrong thing to do. Paul needed to think. He needed reassurance that what he was doing was right.

CHAPTER 6

The old man allowed his mind to drift back to his first, actually second encounter with Reggie Locke… It was just after his entire world had fallen apart. Marsha had been taken, his job had been terminated, and now he had no home at the end of the month. There was a soft knock at the door. It was so quiet Paul thought a small child was probably playing a silly prank on him. "Who's there?" Paul called through the door.

"Reggie Locke, sir."

"I don't know a Reggie Locke. You must have the wrong address."

"No, Professor. I am at the correct location."

Professor? No one called him professor except on the campus. It was strictly forbidden. A title away from the workplace might elevate one in the eyes of the masses. A distinction in one's conduct might be observed, and that was not allowed. Who was this person?

His curiosity got the better of him. He had no choice but to open the door. Paul cautiously eased the door open. No sooner was the door cracked than Reggie was in like a slithering snake. He was fast and calculated. Reggie knew time was not a thing to be wasted. Reggie came straight to the point. "Professor Allen, I know your predicament, and I might be able to help." Paul said nothing. He wasn't about to speak until he knew more. "Sir, I can only trust that what I say will be held in strictest confidence." Paul almost laughed in the young man's face. Nothing was secret. The very walls had ears. Was this young Reggie Locke so naïve as to believe anything or anyone could be trusted except God Himself. "Professor, I am part of a group that has hopes and dreams. Sir, we know that you know."

In that brief instant, all life seemed drained from Paul's body. He grew limp and thought he might faint. He was visibly shaken. He felt his hands tremble. There was no way anyone knew. He had been careful. He had memorized his findings. There was no paper trail. He had even covered the source of his discovery to the point that it was impossible to find. Suddenly, Paul remembered the face of the young man in front of him. He had been in the main office the day of his termination. Now the face had a name, Reggie Locke, but the mystery remained. Paul decided to continue to listen. Maybe this Reggie Locke was talking about something else. "Professor Allen, we need your help. In return we will help you with your problem, or should I say problems." Paul's ears perked. He needed help all right and fast. The hearing to regain custody of Marsha was only a few days away, and with employment and shelter gone, his world seemed bleaker than ever.

Silence continued to rule Paul's end of the conversation. Reggie continued, "Sir, you do not know me. You really don't know if I can be trusted. Likewise, I really don't know if I can trust you. With your permission, I will return tomorrow afternoon. It will simply appear as if I am bringing some of your things from the university. At that time, if you so choose, we will talk. This will give you time to think on what you know. Let me leave you with this thought: You know where it's located. We have the means to get there." With those words, Reggie headed for the door.

The last words of Reggie Locke reverberated through Paul's head. Did this group of which Reggie spoke really believe they could get there? In Paul's mind, it seemed impossible, but he had to find out. Tomorrow—yes, tomorrow—he would find out. Maybe, the truth would not be found in so many words, but he would know.

Paul knew the young man was sizing him up just as he had done. It was all about trust. Reggie Locke needed a day to think just as much as Paul needed that day. After all, if Paul knew too much, he could easily sell out the group, whoever they were. The young man had no way of knowing that honor coursed through his veins. He would never betray Reggie Locke not even if it meant an easier existence for himself, not now, not ever. For Paul, to be disloyal would mean the final loss of his humanity. Yes, he had honor, and he planned on keeping it.

Paul now had to consider long and hard as to whether or not this Reggie Locke was a person of similar character. Usually, Paul was a very good judge of character. He just seemed to know; however, he could not let his guard down. Look at the mess he was in because of the woman at the records office. Yes, but he instinctively knew the woman was not to be trusted. He had no such misgivings about Reggie Locke. It was decided. He would listen and perhaps say a few things. Paul would trust his instincts. Maybe something good would come from his encounter with this Reggie Locke.

Paul's body was tired. He needed to sleep. Tomorrow would be best handled with an alert mind. With those thoughts, sleep closed in on his mind, offering a quiet respite from the troubles of the past few days. Paul wanted plain, unadulterated sleep with no dreams. At last, he got his wish. There were no dreams, only peaceful rest.

The following morning the sun came up bright and full of hope. Perhaps this was a good omen. He had the entire day to think on what should and should not be told. The old what ifs started controlling his thought process. What if Reggie Locke did not really know the secret? What if there was no real way to get there? What if this was just one big joke aimed to embarrass him? Worse yet, what if Reggie Locke never returned?

The day dragged on and on. In addition to Paul's concerns about this new acquaintance, he still did not know where Marsha had been taken. He could only pray that she was safe. He had to find a place to live and fast. This was not going to be easy. Who was going to hire a terminated professor? Paul was taboo. One call to the verification office, and the door would close immediately. Paul would have to make his way in a hostile environment by relying on himself, or so he thought.

At precisely 4:00 p.m., the soft knock came to the door. This time Paul said nothing. Instead, he very quietly opened the door, and Reggie Locke entered. The door was closed and securely locked behind the new acquaintance. Somehow, Paul thought the locked door might keep the conversation from escaping. Paul offered Reggie a seat. Reggie made his way to an oversized, sage-colored chair. The chair had seen its best days, but it still served the purpose for which it was intended. After all, most of the masses would have been happy to have any kind of chair, well worn or not. Reggie took the lead in the conversation. "Have you considered my proposal?"

"Yes, I have."

"What is your answer?"

Paul carefully chose his words. Trust was a tricky emotion to build, and he was treading in unchartered waters with Reggie. "I'm not sure what you think I know, but I certainly need help."

Reggie sensed Paul's caution and answered, "We'll take this partnership nice and slow. In time, if we both possess what I think we do, we will trust each other with our very lives."

The two were on the same wavelength, but it was also apparent that not too much was going to be revealed at this meeting. Reggie finally spoke what was at the top of Paul's priority list. "Your hearing about your daughter comes about in a few days?"

"Yes."

"I don't have to tell you that things look very bad at this point. Your daughter, what's her name?"

"Marsha."

"Marsha will more than likely be removed from your custody."

"Wait a minute. I thought you were going to help."

"Hold on. Let me finish. If this happens, and I strongly expect this to be the case, act the part of an upset parent. Just don't overdo it."

"Mr. Locke."

"Call me Reggie, please."

"Reggie, if that happens, I won't have to act. My emotions will be very real."

"Sir."

"Please dispense with the formalities and call me Paul."

"Paul, our group—"

"Wait, wait, wait! Who is this group to which you refer?"

"Paul, at this time it is not necessary for you to know names. I can tell you we are small in number, but there are group members in places that can actually get things done."

"Then why am I going to lose custody of Marsha?"

"Some things cannot be changed, but the blow can... shall we say... be padded."

"You'll have to explain what you mean."

"If you lose custody of Marsha, she will be placed in a 'special' home. It will be in the home of someone we trust. You will later join her in a trustworthy community. This way you will eventually regain custody of your daughter. Everything will be done secretly and in a very remote location. We will take care of everything. For our help, you will assist us in accomplishing our goal."

"And what might that be?"

"Why, sir." Reggie paused. "Freedom. It's all about being free."

With that answer, the tears gathered in Paul Allen's eyes. The sound of the word had all but been forgotten in his vocabulary, and there it was being uttered by someone he hardly knew. It sounded good. The word was sweetness to his ears. Paul didn't mean for it to happen, but the tears flowed. He couldn't stop the display. Paul glanced at Reggie. He too was crying. It was an emotional moment the two shared. The cornerstone had been laid for the trust that would follow them through thick and thin. Paul was a willing member of the group. The remainder of his life would be devoted to one thing: freedom.

After a while, the tears ceased. Paul led Reggie to the door. Reggie said, "I will not make contact with you until the hearing is complete. Try not to worry. Our member is quite prominent. This person is familiar with your case and will take care of the problem."

For the first time in a long time, Paul dared to trust another human being. In fact, he had trusted no one but God in so long that the experience seemed quite strange. As Paul prepared for bed, recent events caught up with him. He was tired. Yet, he managed to pause and thank God for the events of the day. He at last had hope, not just hope for life after death. He had hope for the human race. Paul Allen slept, and the dreams stayed away.

CHAPTER 7

The old man halted his thoughts of his earlier encounters with Reggie Locke. It had been quite a while since Reggie had contacted him. Paul believed that the time of departure was very close. Maybe, just maybe, the next time Reggie visited he would bring the news he so wanted to hear. This made it all the more urgent that Paul decide how to handle the situation with Marsha. As much as Paul would like to dwell on the future, he had to remember the past…

The day Paul had dreaded for two weeks had finally arrived. He was pretty sure of the outcome. No, he wasn't pretty sure. He was positive about what was to take place. Reggie had gently warned him. How he hoped he could count on Reggie Locke, the mystery man.

The day was bright with plenty of sunshine as he stepped out the door with his bike in tow. At least it wasn't one of those gray days that always lent themselves to real downers. No, the day was filled with an abundance of sun. The weather was warm. The day would have been as perfect as a day could be in the world in which he lived except for the storm cloud of a custody hearing hanging over his head.

As Paul mounted his bike, he noticed that the beautiful weather did not relieve his sense of impending disaster, but still the weather made his ride on the potholed street to the Child Settlement Office bearable. Paul's journey ended in front of a bike rack that was so rusted and in need of repair that he hesitated to leave his only means of transportation, but there was nowhere else to park. Besides, others had left their bikes. Paul surmised that his bike would be okay since it looked a lot worse than some of the others.

Paul then entered the poorly lit building that was no better off today than it had been two weeks earlier. This time Paul headed for the third floor. As he trudged toward the in-need-of-repairs stairway, he passed an out-of-order elevator. The entire building seemed as dilapidated as the people working within its dark walls. Paul slowly climbed the stairs to the door that read "Third Floor." He opened the door and read a sign that said "Hearings" with an arrow pointing to the left. Paul made his way down the dismal hall until he arrived in a room with small cubicles almost stacked on top of one another.

The rather middle-aged woman with a monotone voice said, "Your name."

"Paul Allen."

"Fourth cubicle on the left."

That was all. No interaction. No compassion. Simply five words. With those words, Paul made his way to the tiny cubicle where a thin, long-faced man sat with all the paperwork neatly placed in front of him. "Have a seat."

Paul obeyed without question. The long-faced man began the meeting. "I see your daughter was removed from your care. No cause is given. Of course, as you know, no cause is necessary. The state has decided that your daughter will be better off in another location, one that is perhaps a little more conventional. I need you to sign these papers stating that you attended this meeting and that you understand what has been decided."

"Understand? I understand nothing. Neither she nor I have done anything worthy of being separated. So, maybe you would care to be a little more specific. And, by the way, her name is Marsha!"

"Sir, I haven't the time for this. Your explanation has been given. I must move on to the next hearing."

"This is not a hearing. I have heard nothing that makes me an unfit parent."

"Sir, be calm. We realize this is a delicate matter, but emotion does not accomplish anything."

As the last words blabbered out of the stick man's mouth, Paul reached across the rather small table and yanked the stunned man up by the collar. In that instant Paul could have pulverized him, but he remembered Reggie's words to be upset, just not too upset. Paul slowly released the pathetic-looking man from his grasp. He signed the paper and walked out.

The hallway appeared to stretch forever, the stairway seemed twice as long, the elevator was horribly ancient, and the entire building was a dungeon. The front door appeared to be at least a mile away. Upon reaching the faraway exit, Paul stepped out into what had been a warm day filled with sunshine. Now all he could see was gray clouds although the sun was still brightly shining. His world was upside down. Reggie had warned him, but he still was not prepared for such a charade. Paul walked slowly to the bike rack. His bike was still there. Miracle of miracles, it was still intact. Maybe it was a sign. Marsha was still out there. Paul had to believe that she too was still intact. Paul pulled the bike from the rack and headed to the apartment as fast as he could go. Reggie had said he would contact him after the hearing, and he didn't want to miss him. Paul hoped and prayed that Reggie Locke would contact him soon. Paul only had a few days before he had to vacate his home. Time was of the essence. Paul Allen had been so submissive for so long that he hardly knew where to begin looking for his child, but if Reggie didn't come through and soon, he would find out. Marsha was his and Renee's child, and she was not going to be brought up by a bunch of zombies. Not his child. Not now. Not ever.

CHAPTER 8

Paul was jolted back to the present. "Hey, Gramps! Thought any more about our fishing trip?"

"Oh, yes. We may have to wait until spring. The fishing will be great then. Remember, keep it to yourself. I really haven't spoken with your mom, but I'm sure she'll be okay with it."

With those words, Nat was out the door. He had a lot of energy that needed to be channeled. The old man knew the time to let go of this sanctuary was close. It would be painful at first, but the last thirty years had all been leading to this moment. The old man's mind drifted back to another child, his daughter…

Two days after the meeting with the elites, Paul still had not heard from Reggie. What was taking so long? Impatience gripped every ounce of his being. Paul could not help but believe that a lesson was surely involved in the waiting; however, if patience was the goal, the exercise was being wasted on him.

Walk. That's exactly what Paul needed to do. Out the door he went. The fresh air slapped him in the face. He became keenly aware of how long he had been cooped in the apartment. Somehow, it didn't seem to matter that he might miss Reggie. Hope had begun to fade. Perhaps, he had trusted the wrong person. No, he did not believe that. Paul had an instinct when it came to people, and Reggie Locke could be trusted. Something was simply taking longer than Reggie had anticipated.

Paul suddenly felt that he was being followed. He moved at a brisker pace. The suspected henchman moved faster as well. Finally the person spoke. "Don't turn around."

Paul recognized the voice to be that of Reggie Locke. "What took you so long to leave that apartment?"

Paul replied, "I didn't want to miss you."

"I couldn't come. I feared someone might be watching your home. I thought it best to wait for you to come out. Listen carefully. I'm going to bump into you and drop a small piece of paper in your pocket. Finish your walk just as you had planned. Then go home. Do not read the note until you get inside your apartment. Follow the instructions carefully. Everything is in place to reunite you with your daughter."

Paul felt a strong push from the back. "Excuse me, sir. I'm so sorry. I wasn't watching where I was going."

With that, Reggie was gone. Shortly thereafter, he was completely out of sight. Paul took a few more steps. He straightened his clothes and in a very discreet way checked his pants pocket. There it was safe and tucked away. He could hardly wait to get back to the apartment that just a few minutes ago he couldn't wait to exit. In spite of the anxious feelings, he managed to walk at least a mile before heading home.

Upon arriving, he fumbled with the lock. Any other day, it would have opened so quickly he would have wondered if the door was truly locked, but today he was nervous. That note held his and Marsha's future, and he was once again hopeful. Strange how returning hope always seems stronger. Yes, at this moment, he felt his life was starting over or at least being rejuvenated. Finally, the door opened. Paul rushed to the bedroom and turned on a dim light. He pulled the paper from his pocket. It read:

> On the last day of the month, ride your bike west to the bridge on the outskirts of town. Be there at 10:00 a.m. There will be a man standing on the bridge looking out over the water. Stop, get off your bike, and join him about six feet from where he is standing. After a while, he will say, "The doves are restless today." You will reply, "The cats are prowling." Shortly thereafter, he will leave in the direction from which you came. After ten minutes, continue westward on your bike. Travel one mile, and you will see a dirt road on your left. Turn in and go about one-half mile. The man from the bridge will be waiting for you with further instructions. Before leaving your home, you must destroy all personal papers. This includes pictures, birth certificates, marriage papers, yes, even family Bibles. There is, however, one set of papers you must keep. We believe you to be in possession of some documents that your grandmother gave you

> long ago. Bring those. Hide them in your clothes in such a way that the bulk does not show. Memorize these instructions and destroy this note.

With his memory, Paul already had the note committed, but he was puzzled. How did these people know about the documents, much less how he came to have them? How did they know about G? He would search for the answers to those questions later. For right now, he was thankful to have an ally, someone who would help unite him with his daughter.

There was much to be done. The last day of the month was tomorrow, and he had so much to be burned. How he hated to destroy the little things that gave record to his existence. Paul started a small fire in his only trash can. He felt he was destroying a part of himself as each picture was examined, the details memorized, and the evidence burned. When Paul came to the picture of Blubber, he could not burn it. The photograph represented freedom. Paul slipped the picture in his pocket closest to his heart and continued the destruction. After the great burning, all he would have would be the picture of the huge fish and the memories. After the pictures were turned to wispy ashes, he brought out the certificates. One by one, they became victims of the fire. At last, he came to the piece of paper that he so hated to part with… his marriage papers. He looked over the document. How he still missed Renee, and yet there was something very final about throwing their life together into the fire. But he must. Tears streamed down his cheeks as he held the neatly folded paper close to his heart. Paul thought, *Forgive me, Renee. I will always think of you, but I must protect our daughter.* With that thought, Paul gently placed the paper on the glowing remnants of the fire. Flames immediately erupted, and all but the memories were gone.

The last item Paul chose to burn was the family Bible. Not only did he feel shame at the very idea of burning records that were entrusted to him, he felt guilt at allowing the sinister flames to touch the very Word of God. Bibles were in short supply, and he was going to burn one of the precious few left. When G had purchased the Bible, Bibles were in abundance. Before ripping the pages out a few at a time, he turned to the back cover. His mom had showed him the secret compartment many years ago. The salesman had made a pitch about how precious things could be stored in the rather thin pouch. Locks of children's hair, a precious letter, or small things with significance could easily be placed in the niche. Yet, somehow G had managed to store several documents in the small area. She must have folded and refolded to make the items fit perfectly so that no one would ever suspect the contents. The only Bibles that could be kept in homes were those for family records. The elites deemed the records to be of great importance. The Word of God was an extra that the elites didn't believe anyone would bother with anyway. How naïve the elites were. The Word of God had given many a family the strength to overcome the trials this evil society had placed on them. Yet to the elites the family records were all that were important. Now, Paul was about to destroy those records along with God's precious Word. Paul gently removed the faux binding. He could not remember how many times through the years the elites had looked at the Bible but never found the secret compartment. Bibles had to be registered, and they were thoroughly examined before registration was granted. Yet the elites never suspected a thing. Paul then carefully laid back the cardboard back. There they were in a neat, flat arrangement, not a stack, but methodically placed. Paul removed the thin papers. He wouldn't have to concern himself with showing bulk through his clothes. The papers would easily fit into a pocket on his pants. Paul laid the papers to the side and reverently tore a few pages of the Bible at a time and once again fed the embers. By the time he was finished, he was so laden with guilt that he felt heavy from the burden. Paul was thankful when the destruction was finished.

Tonight Paul would rest. Tomorrow would be a new day. Soon he would be reunited with his daughter. He would be thrilled to see Marsha. He could only imagine that she had grown quite a bit since their separation. Yes, tomorrow life would be better.

CHAPTER 9

"Gramps, Gramps, come here! Come here quick!" The old man was snatched from his world of thought.

"What is it, son?"

"Come quick!"

The old man raced to the front window and slowly pulled the corner of the curtain back. It became very obvious what was creating Nat's panic. A truck had entered their community. That by itself did not cause the uproar, but armed men jumped out of the bed of this truck. The intended abductors started immediately rounding up the able-bodied men in the village. Anyone between the ages of eighteen and fifty was ordered at gunpoint to climb into the truck. According to the thieves, the men were needed in service to the cause. What cause? All worthy causes had been abandoned years ago. The old man thought, *Things must be getting pretty tense for these people to come to this remote place and steal people.* An episode such

as this had not happened in at least ten years. Paul had to do something. These were people with whom he had lived for nearly thirty years. "Nat, stay here. I need to go out alone. Do not follow. Maybe I can stop this senseless disaster from happening."

Nat watched as his gramps grabbed his cane and hobbled toward the door. Gramps ordered Nat, "Do not come out. No matter what, stay here."

Reluctantly, Nat stayed behind, but he watched. He was not sure what one old man could accomplish against big, strong men, but he had faith that Gramps could move mountains if that's what he decided to do. Nat saw Gramps speaking to what must have been the leader. Arms were raised, fingers were pointed back and forth, and voices were elevated though Nat could not hear what was being said. Finally, all the men on the truck were free to go to their homes. The armed thugs climbed in their truck and headed out to the main road. At last, Gramps returned to the house. Nat was full of questions. "What happened? Why did they leave? Are they coming back? What did they want?"

"It seems there was some unrest in the east, and they were needing recruits. I don't think they'll be coming back for a while."

"Why not?" Nat asked.

"I explained to them that we are experiencing an outbreak of smallpox and most of the community has been exposed."

"Are we really?"

"No, no, no. Your mom and I have always taught you to be truthful, but I had to protect these people as best that I could." Paul knew in a very short while these people would have to fend for themselves. He had always known that someday he would be leaving. He had supposed that he would just ease out to the main road one day, and life would go on as usual. That no longer appeared to be the case. Those thugs would return. It might be a month. It might even be a year, but eventually they would return. They knew how many were here. They knew the lay of the land. They may have been stupid in many ways, but they were smart, very smart when it came to creating chaos in the lives of others. "Nat, we're okay for now. It's okay to go outside with your friends. I need to rest a few minutes."

Nat was thankful to head outside. He wanted to hear what everyone was saying. Paul heard the door slam. The old man needed to think about how he had come to this wonderful group of people. These were people who had taken him in when he was little more than a vagabond. They asked few questions. They simply trusted that those strangers among them would not betray them. They were indeed the salt of the earth. These people were what made life tolerable. They were intelligent. They were self-sufficient. Maybe it was the fresh air, maybe the hard work, or maybe the isolation that made them a strong group. Whatever it was, the old man could not leave them behind to suffer the consequences of his lie. The smallpox story had sent the thugs trotting for the time being, but they would return. Paul feared for his friends. He would have to be sure they had an escape plan before he could leave. In his quest for freedom, he did not want to lose his humanity.

The old man's mind wandered back to the time when he was leaving his old life and entering his new life with these precious people. It was a lifetime ago. Paul was different now, older, wiser, but far more vulnerable. He now had more than Marsha to consider. There was Nat, and now he felt responsible for the well-being of a whole community. He had to think. He had to remember the events that had led him to this village. The old man's thoughts went back to the day of his departure and the days leading to his arrival in the community…

Paul left his apartment for the last time about nine thirty a.m. on a day filled with sunshine and oddly enough hope as well. It was indeed strange how nature reached out to offer calmness when the entire world seems to be in turbulence. Such was this day. Beautiful it was. Paul even heard the birds chirping. He noticed a squirrel scampering into the half-dead oak tree in front of the complex. Had Marsha been with him, he would have pointed out the obvious to her, and she would have been delighted as only a child could be. Yes, there was hope.

Paul grabbed his bike, threw his leg across the bar, and headed west to the bridge at the edge of town. Upon arriving, he noticed a man gazing into the river below. The water moved slowly along. Nothing was about to interrupt its journey. Gently the river made its way around the bend, never stopping, always moving. Paul parked his bike and stood about six feet from the man. He was unsure of what to do next. After all, he really had not known what or who to expect. Somehow this man did not fit his expectations. He was young, very young, and he did not seem at all interested in Paul's presence. Finally, without even looking in Paul's direction, the man said, "The doves are restless today."

To which, Paul tried not to act shocked as he calmly replied, "The cats are prowling."

The man waited for what seemed an eternity. He then turned, got on his bike, and headed toward town. It was a long ten minutes before Paul mounted his bike and headed farther out of town. A bike can cover a mile in a short length of time if one is getting away from an undesirable situation. It can be ridden even faster if one does not want to run the risk of being seen. Such was Paul's case. Paul pedaled with all his strength and soon turned onto the dirt road. The half-mile took longer because the road was little more than a path with deep ruts that were to be avoided. At last, he saw the same man sitting under a stately maple tree. Paul dismounted and joined the young man. The man spoke first. "Sir, it is my pleasure to see you once again."

Paul looked puzzled. He studied the young man's face. "Adam Crane. You were in one of my classes two semesters ago."

"Yes, I can tell you I have never been as motivated to learn as when I was in your class. Professor, I would thoroughly enjoy talking with you at great length, but time is short. I must give you instructions and explain things to you. Sir, I too am part of the small group of which Reggie Locke is a member. You, sir, are our only hope."

Paul could almost see desperation on the young man's face as he continued. "Professor, we know that you know where it can be found, and we have the means to get there." The words were almost identical to those of Reggie Locke. "When we reunite you with your daughter, you will help us, won't you?"

Paul had never considered anything else, but he could certainly see how the matter needed to be confronted. Paul answered in a very matter-of-fact way, "I am a man of my word. You can count on me. I will not let you down."

"Sorry, sir, but I had to ask. Without your expertise, our plan will be a failure. We will have only one chance, and everything must come together precisely."

"It will be my pleasure to work with you. Together, perhaps we can make a difference." His words could only be considered an understatement. If they had what Paul believed them to possess, it would be world changing for some.

"Professor."

"Please, call me Paul."

"Sir, after having you as a teacher, it may take a while to call you by your first name, but I'll try. Paul, when you leave me, you will walk back to the main road, continue heading away from town. After about an hour, a covered truck will pull alongside of you. The driver's exact words will be, 'Heavy on your feet?' Your reply will be, 'Light as a feather.' You will then crawl into the back of the truck and place yourself under things so that you will not be easily discovered should the truck be stopped. You will be taken to a commune of sorts that is about a two-day drive from here. There will be plenty of food and water in the back of the truck. When you arrive at the compound, you will be greeted by the commune's leader, Zack Beard. He will show you where you will be living, and your daughter will be there waiting for you. There is, however, a small catch."

"And what might that be?"

"To the people in the commune, you will be Gabe Lawson, and your daughter will be Resa Lawson."

"What?"

"I'm sorry, sir, but for now that's the way it has to be. You see, all records of Paul Allen and daughter Marsha have been destroyed. Sir, you never existed."

Paul was visibly shaken, and it took a moment for him to collect his thoughts. "Adam, I will help in any way I can, but I will always be Paul Allen. My daughter will always be Marsha Allen. The folks in the commune can call me whatever they choose, but my identity is mine. This regime has taken so much from me, but it will not take my soul. My name is a part of my very being. So that a plan can be formulated, I will be Gabe Lawson to the villagers, but my name as it relates to what I hope will be our cause will always be Paul Allen. I will not betray my ancestors, not now, not ever. Is this understood?"

A hush filled the air. It was as if all nature stood still awaiting the response. There was only one answer to the question, and both men knew what it was. The accompanying dialogue was as definite as the placement of the sun, moon, and stars. There would be no change. There would be no negotiating. Paul's resolve was as immoveable as the tallest mountain. It was strong, firm. Paul Allen knew who he was and from where he had come. A line had been drawn in the sand, and Paul dared anyone to cross it. He was Paul Allen, widower of Renee Allen, father of Marsha Allen. He was from a line of brave people, not famous, but some of the most courageous humans to ever walk the face of the earth. He had seen their heroic feats. He had watched, and now he would emulate. He was a product of the past. Of this he was sure… he would be Paul Allen forever.

Adam Crane had no choice but to answer, "Understood." A few brief seconds hung in the air as the conversation settled on both of them. At last Adam continued, "Time for you to start walking."

"What about my bike?"

"I'm going to throw it in the edge of the water. If someone finds it and identifies it as yours, it will be assumed that you had enough and committed suicide. Now, be on your way and best of luck."

Paul started walking down the rough road. Suddenly he stopped and turned on his heels, "When will I see you again?"

"It will probably be about two years. The state has decided that I need another two years in which to further my education. I certainly wish I were studying under you, Professor."

Paul couldn't resist asking, "I take it you are placing emphasis on math and science?"

"What else is there?"

"Good answer."

On a more serious note, Adam said, "The road ahead requires that all those involved have as much expertise as is possible. I'm sure you agree."

"Agreed." Paul took a few steps toward Adam and firmly grasped his hand. "Until we meet again."

"I look forward to seeing you in two years. Good-bye, Professor."

With that said, Paul headed to the main road and walked away from town. The midday sun beat on his head, but he scarcely noticed. After all, he was on his way to a new life with his daughter.

The hour passed rather quickly as Paul's mind tried to wrap itself around the events of the past few days. How he hoped the group was for real. How he prayed the group had the means to go where he could take them. Suddenly, Paul heard a rumble in the distance. It must be the truck. The noise got closer and closer. Paul turned to see a rather old truck pull up beside him. The driver looked out the window and asked, "Heavy on your feet?"

Paul replied without hesitation, "Light as a feather."

The driver gave a quick point to the back of the truck. Paul raced to the hung-down tarp and pulled it back. He jumped up to the edge and thrust himself inside. As he felt the truck lunge forward, he quickly found a place in the front corner to cover up and hide. On his way to the hiding place, he noticed the truck had several crates of fresh fruit and vegetables. No doubt he would have plenty to eat. As Paul settled in, he grew very tired. He fell off to sleep and rested, actually rested. He had not done that in weeks. He felt at peace. Somehow, someway, everything was going to be okay.

CHAPTER 10

Paul did not know how long he had been asleep, but it must have been quite a while. When he awoke, it was dark, very dark. Paul felt the truck slow. He knew he had not slept all the way to his destination, so he could only assume they had arrived at a checkpoint. Paul was confident that he was well hidden. Perhaps they would not even look in the back of the truck. The truck slowly stopped. Paul listened for voices. A booming voice pierced the darkness, "Get out of the truck."

Paul heard the door of the truck open. He felt the truck sway as the driver stepped out. The booming voice told the driver, "Pull back the curtain." Paul dared not breathe.

The driver obeyed the voice and said, "As you can see, I am carrying only fresh fruits and vegetables to our community. I am about a half-day's drive from home."

The booming voice must have been satisfied. He said, "You may go. Here's your checkpoint receipt just in case you're stopped again between here and your destination."

"Thank you. I appreciate this very much."

Paul felt the weight of the man move the truck slightly as he climbed into the cab. He heard the door shut just as the motor cranked up. The truck pushed forward, and they were moving again. Paul at last could breathe deeply. He was only a half day from seeing his daughter. Even with the just past danger, Paul smiled. He didn't know when, much less how, but life was going to be different, a good different.

The remainder of the trip was rather uneventful, and about noon of the following day, Paul felt the truck slow and turn right onto what seemed to be a gravel road. The air felt fresh. He must be in a rural area. It had been a long time since he had felt air this fresh. Even inside the truck on a dusty, gravel road, Paul could tell the difference. People reared in the country knew the difference. This was definitely some out-of-the-way place, and that was just fine with him.

After about ten minutes of bumping along, the truck came to a halt. Paul dared not move until told to do so. Minutes passed that seemed like hours. Finally, light broke through the edge of the truck's tarp. "Gabe, Gabe Lawson?"

"I'm right here," Paul answered as he tried to stand after having been curled in a ball for many hours.

"Come on out."

Paul made his way to the rear of the truck, where he was helped down by a man who introduced himself as Zack Beard. "We're glad to have you here. We hope your stay will be a pleasant one." Zack left no room for conversation. Everything was stated in a rather rehearsed way. Something told Paul that this was not the first introduction to be made by Zack Beard. Though much younger than Paul, Zack appeared to be the leader of the community. Zack continued, "We have few rules here, but the ones we observe are to be adhered to by everyone. All people work here. There are no handouts. Life is hard, and we pull together. Given what we know about you and your daughter—"

Paul jumped. Marsha must be here. Paul was still listening, but he was getting impatient. He wanted to make sure Marsha was in one piece. He wanted to see that she was as okay as a child could be after having been ripped from her father's care.

"We want you to teach at the school. We have few qualified facilitators here, and to have one who is certified in math and science is a real honor. You will be shown to your dwelling shortly. It's nothing fancy, but it is comfortable. As time goes by, I'm sure you will fit very nicely into our community."

"Thank you for allowing me to come into your community. You may have to help me adjust to your way of doing things, but I can assure you that I will conform as quickly as possible."

With the necessary formalities out of the way, Zack introduced Paul to Ned, "Gabe, this is Ned Brook. He will show you where you will be staying. He and his family have been caring for Resa until your arrival. I'm sure you're ready to get settled in."

Paul could barely contain himself. Marsha was here, and she must be okay. If not, surely he would have detected something in Zack's voice. There would certainly have been some telltale sign that he would have recognized. A slight inflection of the voice, eyes looking off at something that wasn't there, shuffling feet, a loss of words, but nothing unusual was there. Paul surmised this to mean that his daughter was at the least okay.

Paul and Ned shook hands. Ned said, "I'm glad you're here. Understand you're a teacher. We're always happy to get good people here. I can tell from being around your daughter that you're good people. She acts like she's been reared, not yanked up by the hair of her head. You should be proud of her, Gabe. To be separated from her dad could not have been easy, but she's a trooper. I have a daughter her age. In the past few days, they've become good friends."

"Oh, so you have one daughter, also."

"Yes, she was one of the secrets." Paul looked puzzled. "You see, I have a twelve-year-old son as well. Out in the middle of nowhere you can sometimes get things by the state. When Susie, my wife, discovered she was pregnant, we almost panicked. We were afraid the elites' thugs would show up and do, well, no telling what." Paul understood the justification for the couple's fear. Ned continued, "Instead, the thugs stayed away almost a year. You see, Gabe, when the secrets happen, we have a plan. The extra babies are always claimed by a childless couple or a single person who never plans to marry. It works, and no one is worse for wear. If people's circumstances change, the story changes. After all, it's not like the thugs come to stay. They come to let us know they are out there. Occasionally, a group of elites come. I think they like to look down their pointed noses at us. We're polite to them, and soon they leave. Make no mistake, Gabe, life is hard here. But we're much happier than we would be in a more urban setting."

The two walked as they talked. Paul wanted to learn all he could before arriving at his dwelling. "Zack said there were a few rules. What are they?"

"Number one rule is we abide by the Ten Commandments. With Bibles in such short supply, we've had to pretty much commit them to memory. We make sure our children learn the commandments in school. That's another advantage to living way out here. There's only been a few times when the elites have even asked us about our learning environment. When they have, we invite them to the schoolhouse, which they immediately decline. There are a few copies of the commandments scattered around the commune, but they are well hidden. We also teach our children to abide by the elites' daily rituals. There's no point in asking for trouble."

"Any other rules?"

"Nope. We haven't felt the need for any other rules. We figure if those rules were good enough for God, they'll be good enough for us."

With that said, the two men walked on. Paul knew he and Marsha were going to be just fine. Life evidently would be hard, but they would survive. Paul allowed himself to think, *Sometimes that's all you can hope for in a world without a lot of hope to go around.*

The two men stopped in front of a small building. "This is where you'll be living. It's not much, but as time goes on, we try to make improvements to homes."

Paul assured Ned, "It will be just fine."

The two stepped inside. The building appeared much larger on the inside than it had looked on the outside. There was a small sitting room. A small sofa and rocking chair occupied the room. A table sat between the sofa and chair. Both were facing a fireplace that looked as if it had been recently cleaned. To the right, a small kitchen was equipped with a table and two chairs. Paul immediately noticed a kitchen sink with faucets. "Indoor plumbing?" Paul asked.

"Oh yes, all homes have hot and cold water."

Paul saw a short hallway with a door at the end. Two doors opened opposite each other on either side of the hall. "A bathroom?" Paul further questioned.

"Indeed, along with two bedrooms."

Paul looked at the bedrooms. Each had a bed, nightstand, and chest. In the corner of each was a small closet. The door at the end of the hall held a small bathroom. Everything was small, but clean. He and Marsha would certainly be able to survive nicely in this environment. They would ask for nothing. They would contribute whatever resources they had to this community. And when the time came to leave, they would leave the place as good or better than they had found it. That's how Paul Allen had been raised, and he was not about to change. Of that, he was sure.

Paul turned to Ned. "I appreciate all you've done for us. How can I ever thank you?"

"No thanks are needed. Just be a good schoolteacher. Oops, my age is showing. I mean just be a good facilitator. That will be thanks enough."

"I'll do my best."

Just as the words rolled from his mouth, the door burst open, and in popped a sight for sore eyes… Paul's daughter with her new friend, Priscilla. "Dad, where did you come from? I had no idea you were here. Why didn't someone tell me you were coming?"

Questions didn't seem to need answers as Marsha leapt into the arms of her dad. She gave him hugs and kisses all over his face. And, of course, they were freely returned. At last, Paul released the child from his hold. Marsha stepped back, and Paul said, "My goodness, you look like you've grown three inches."

"Actually, I've grown one inch."

"I'm so glad to see you, sweetie."

"Me too!"

"Was everyone nice to you?"

"Well, the first place I went they were a little crabby, but it was okay."

"How many places have you been?"

"This one makes four. The second place I don't think liked children. They wanted complete and total silence. I didn't like that much." Paul could only imagine what a hardship that had been. "I only stayed there two days. The third place I went to was a nice place. Dad, they had a dog. Can you believe that? They had a real dog. Dad, you know what else?"

"No, what?"

"They had three children."

"Three?"

"Three. Dad, they had triplets, and they were my age. I had fun, but not as much fun as I've had here." She glanced at Priscilla. "Dad, can we please stay here?"

"As far as I'm concerned, this is home." Paul looked in the direction of Ned.

Ned said, "We're glad to have you." With those words spoken, Ned and Priscilla headed toward the door. "I'll send Priscilla and Nathaniel over with Resa's things just as soon as they finish their chores."

"No need to do that. Why don't we walk over with you, and Resa and I will bring them back."

"Fine with me."

It was only a short walk to the Brooks' dwelling. The girls ran ahead and delighted in things only children can. Paul broke the silence. "Is this commune safe?"

"Safe? How?"

"I know you said the elites leave you alone most of the time, but have they ever shown any interest in this place?"

"They like to keep up with our numbers. I guess they don't want us to get too large or strong. We know that, and if necessary, our numbers may be off a little. So far, no one seems to care. We try not to give them any reason to question us."

"Sounds like a winning strategy."

As they arrived at the Brooks' household, Paul noticed their dwelling was very similar to his and Marsha's. It might have been a little larger because it had a third bedroom. The group did not like to have homes with three bedrooms. It was one of those things that could make a visiting elite ask questions. But, of course, if that happened, an elderly member of the community would suddenly become a member of the questioned household. Paul and Ned entered the front door and were greeted by Susie, who was busily preparing supper. "Why, Ned

Brook, where's your manners. Are you going to introduce me to your new friend?"

"Susie, this is Resa's dad, Gabe Lawson. Gabe, my wife, Susie."

"Pleased to meet you, Gabe. I'd shake your hand, but you'd look like a powder puff with all this flour on my hands."

"Don't worry about it. I'd like to thank you both for taking such good care of Mar… Resa."

Susie said, "We loved having her. I'm very happy that everything has worked out to where the two of you are together again. We're always around if you need help for any reason. I think you'll see most of the people living here are more than willing to be good neighbors. We've learned to depend on each other for survival, and it works."

"I appreciate your kind offer. Resa's mother passed a while back, so from time to time, I may need a little help bringing up a daughter."

"Any time. Won't you and Resa stay for supper. I know you're tired, and we have plenty."

"You've been more than generous. We couldn't further impose on you."

"Nonsense. It's settled. I'll set two more places."

Ned turned to Paul and said, "While Susie's finishing up, come with me, and I'll show you around."

"Be back in thirty minutes," Susie called as they headed out the door.

Out in the open, Paul marveled at what the community had been able to create with very few resources. The town was laid out in such a way that the dwellings circled the hub of life in the community, which was, of course, the church disguised as a general merchandise store. Next to the church was the school. Everything was orderly. There was no confusion. A live and let live attitude permeated the air, and Paul knew that for now he was at home. This was the best life had to offer, and he wasn't refusing. Paul had heard of places such as this, but this was his first encounter with communal living. It wasn't the freedom of which he was searching, but it would suffice until a better plan was orchestrated.

"What do you think, Gabe?" Ned asked.

"I think it's home. It sure looks like a good place to bring up a family. This place is far from the city, and that seems very good to me."

"Yes, we want to be as far from interference as we can get. Even at that, we still have visits from the elites. Every now and then, they want to remind us of who's the boss. We go along with them and try not to create a stir. In turn, they usually don't stay very long. We always know what to do when they arrive. It's like a rehearsed script. The children know, if asked, who their parents are at that particular moment. In the near future, we'll go over everything with you. You never know. They could arrive at any time with no warning. We'd better head back. We don't want to keep Susie waiting. She's a fine cook and even finer wife. I'm a lucky man."

"Yes, you are," was all Paul could get out. Oh how he still missed Renee, but even with the pain, he was sure Renee would have approved his course of action. Renee was like that… do what you've got to do and accept the results.

As they approached Ned's home, Marsha ran to him and once again jumped into his arms. "I'm so glad we're here, Dad. I love my new home."

"I do too, sweetheart. We are two very fortunate people."

"Yes, we are. Miss Susie is a good cook. You'll love eating here."

"I'm sure I will," Paul replied as he held Marsha close.

Marsha and Ned had not exaggerated. The meal was as good as he had eaten in many months, but it was finally time to go to their new home. It was time for Paul and Marsha to establish themselves in the community. As Paul started for the door, he turned and thanked Ned and Susie once again for taking such good care of Marsha. Then he turned to Marsha, "Want to ride on my back all the way home?"

"Dad, you know I'm too big for that." She paused and quickly added, "But I'll race you home," as she bolted out the door.

Paul quickly said good night and grabbed Marsha's few possessions. Out the door he pursued his daughter. At last Paul felt at peace. It had been weeks since he had been free of his heavy burden, but now he felt as light as air as he raced his daughter to their new home. Even as Paul ran, his mind paused for a moment to give thanks to God for his blessings. How appropriate thankfulness seemed. Paul's life at this point had undergone a transformation. He would never be the same. Father and daughter arrived at the dwelling almost simultaneously with Marsha conveniently a step ahead. As they opened the door, they were again amazed. The little cottage had electricity too. Paul later learned the entire village was running off of a huge generator. "Always remember, Marsha, we want to be good citizens in this community. So the first thing we want to do is use only one light after dark. We do not want to be wasteful."

"Oh, I know, Dad. Mrs. Susie explained everything like that to me. This is a wonderful place."

With those words, the two went inside, climbed in bed, and fell asleep. Life was definitely on the right track. Circumstances could change so quickly, but for now, this was their station in life. They could ask for no more.

CHAPTER 11

Paul was brought back to the present as the door creaked open. He knew instinctively that it was Nat. Maybe it was the soft footsteps or perhaps the feeling that someone was watching him that betrayed the young boy. Either way, Nat slipped right past him. "Mom," Nat softly called as he headed for his mother's room. "Mom, guess what? Everybody says Gramps is the bravest man in the whole world."

"And who is everybody?"

"The whole village."

"Well, he is, isn't he?"

"Yep, he sure is."

Paul could detect pride in Nat's voice. How he hoped he would never let the boy down. The old man could start the "what if" game, but it would change nothing. The course had been set. After all these years, there would be no turning back. There would be one chance.

Failure was not an option. The plan would work. It had to succeed. The future of civilized mankind depended upon the operation. He would have to make Marsha understand. The letters no longer seemed the path to forge. His intuition had been correct about the letters. They were a coward's way out. If he, Paul Allen, was the bravest man in the whole world, surely he could muster the strength to speak with Marsha face to face. He would make her understand. But to make Marsha understand, he would have to reveal more of himself than anyone, not even Renee, knew. He would have to dredge the far corners of his mind. Paul would have to open doors and hope he could close them after the revelations. He knew from the nightmares that doors didn't always close tight, but by waking up, he always managed to push the door closed. To tell Marsha everything, he would be inviting reality to the forefront. But he, Paul Allen—the bravest man in the world—could do it. After revealing the ugliness he had experienced, he would then have to convince Marsha that a better life could be had. This might be far more difficult than the horror stories because Marsha had stories of her own, and he knew hers. She was a brave woman, a determined woman. Life had made her tougher than leather. He would have to make her see things his way. If he could do that, he would have no greater ally than Marsha.

Marsha had met Reggie Locke as a child. After his visits, she always seemed to have a puzzled look on her face that said, "Who is this man?" Reggie would weigh heavily in his argument for their departure. Paul thought about Reggie's earliest visits…

Paul and Marsha had been living in the community about six months when, just as promised, Reggie Locke showed up. He didn't create any great excitement. No one seemed at all surprised when he made his way to Paul's home. Paul and Marsha had made themselves fit in to the point that no one even thought of them as just passing through. This was their home. This was their routine. They assumed the live-and-let-live philosophy of the group, and as a result, they were accepted. Paul taught math and science to the older children in the daytime, and after school he helped the men of the village do whatever needed to be done. One day he might help plant corn. The next he might be milking cows. He didn't mind. Marsha was in the same school with him. He knew what she was being taught. There was no indoctrination of the virtues of the state. Instead, she was actually learning the basics of a good education. She was blossoming as a student. While he was helping with the chores, Susie watched Marsha. It was a win-win arrangement. These people shared his values. He was one of them. No matter where his path took him, this was home. He was as much at home as he had been as a child on the farm. He truly felt that nothing could change his perspective until the arrival of Reggie Locke.

When Reggie knocked at the door, Paul immediately answered it. Upon seeing Reggie, Paul had an "it's time to pay up" feeling. Not a bad feeling, instead, it was a belief that things were about to take a turn. "Come in, friend. It's been a while," Paul greeted Reggie.

"Yes, it has. Thought I'd drop by and see how things were going."

"I can't thank you enough for finding us a place here. Life is hard, but it's a good life. Of course, everyone knows there's a dangerous world out there that could change at any moment which in turn could set this place upside down." There it was. He had said it. No matter what kind of life the group was experiencing, there was still a world out there determining their fate. This was not good. Reggie's very presence made Paul focus on the big picture, and he didn't like what he was forced to confront. He was a temporary resident of this community. Reggie had come to discuss matters of great importance.

"Sir, are we alone?"

"No, Marsha is in her room."

"Is there someplace she can go?"

Paul called to his daughter, "Sweetie, would you mind going to Mrs. Susie's and visiting Priscilla and Nathaniel for a while." Paul knew that would be her biggest delight of the day. She loved the Brook family, and they loved her. "I'll come for you after a while."

Marsha hugged her dad as she headed out the door. Paul watched as Marsha skipped down the path. Paul loved how he never had to worry about letting his child go to a neighbor's home. Everyone knew everyone. They watched out for each other. The children were precious in the eyes of the village, and no child was ever very far from the caring eyes of someone. When Marsha was out of sight, Paul returned his focus to his guest. "What can I do for you?"

"It's time to set our plan in motion. That is if we have a plan."

"What makes you think I know anything? I have always stayed in the background, never caused any great waves until recently."

"Paul, do you remember a Professor Eric Locke?"

"I don't think so."

"How about a conference you attended several years ago about the body's reaction to heat?"

Paul laughed. "Was that silly or what?" Suddenly the laughter halted. The topic was no longer humorous. That was what the dumbing down of America had done. Academic challenges were over. "Yes, I remember. Professor Locke was the guest speaker. He was quite interesting given the subject matter."

Reggie somberly replied, "He was my father."

"Was?"

"He died a few years ago."

"I'm sorry."

"Dad had a longing for the same things we hope to achieve."

Paul quizzically asked, "And what might that be?"

"Dad wanted a better life free of those in control." Paul could hear a hint of anger in Reggie's voice.

"How might we achieve this better life?"

"There's only one way. We must leave, and you, sir, know where we're going. Don't try to deny it. You didn't realize it, but Dad was watching you the night you discovered the place where we can settle."

Paul sat silently. There was nothing to say. How could this be? He had been so careful. All Paul had meant to do that night was play with the computers. Old though they were, they were still far more advanced than anything to which he had been accustomed. When capitalism failed… no, *failed* was not the word. Capitalism never failed. It was simply replaced. When capitalism was replaced with socialism, the entrepreneurial spirit was replaced as well. It wasn't too long before advanced technology was gone. Civilization was stuck with remnants of the past. Paul had simply wanted to see what he could make those computers do. Quite by accident, there it was on the screen. He couldn't believe his eyes. The following day he returned to the computer lab. This time he had no trouble locating what he was after. What he did notice was that it seemed to be fading, almost trying to hide. Quickly Paul memorized the coordinates. They were in his mind, but he knew he couldn't chance an error. He decided the coordinates must be preserved in a place where only he could find them. The next day the location was back, bright and clear. Paul knew that he had to make sure no one ever discovered his findings. He didn't know much about this particular machine, but he knew he could lose every remnant of what he had discovered. A few adjustments were made, and it was done. Not even he could find it. Paul was sure that he had been alone each time. The thought process had caused Paul to realize that it was best not to deny the truth. The days of cat and mouse were at an end. Paul sensed Reggie was speaking the truth. He wasn't bluffing. Paul would have to trust, just not completely at this point. Paul quietly asked, "Where was he?"

"Oh, he wasn't in the same room. Part of his job was to keep an eye on some of the attendees. You were assigned to him. He noticed you were spending quite a bit of time in the computer lab, so he decided to check out what was holding your interest. After one of your trips to the lab, he was able to see what you were viewing. At first, the picture seemed quite muddled. Then it disappeared. He saw it, Paul. Just like you, he saw it. He was never able to find it again. In fact, it was several days before he fully realized what he had seen. By then, you had wiped the slate clean. His mission became to secure a way to go there. Paul, he succeeded. On his deathbed, he told me the story. Some of his last words were, 'Find Paul Allen.' Sir, that's how I came to be at the university where you taught. Dad told me that you knew where to go."

"I do." With those two words Paul had committed to what he had dared to hope but never dreamed attainable. The two men smiled. They were like two boys who had just taken cookies without permission. They felt sneaky. They were determined to beat the unjust system that had been thrust upon them. They would match wits with the low life of their world, and they were sure they would win. "How soon?"

Reggie's smile faded. Paul could read from his expression that the conversation was about to take a serious turn. Paul slowly repeated the question. This time Paul could hear a touch of desperation in his own voice. "How soon?"

"There are details that we must discuss. You see, we have the means to get us there, but there are unfinished areas of our vessel."

"How unfinished?"

"If we could just go in and finish the project, I'd say one year, but each detail has to be stretched into a very long, time-consuming plan. Paul, we are very unsure of the time frame."

"You mean it could be years?"

"I'm afraid so."

"What if we don't have years to leave this place?"

"We must be careful. One careless move in front of the wrong people, and there could be no escape mechanism. Sir, care must be practiced on all levels."

"I understand and appreciate what you're saying, but surely the process can move faster than a snail's pace."

"Paul, it hasn't been easy finding people with the expertise to accomplish our goals. This vessel was mothballed long ago, so there are very few people alive who understand the inner-workings of the ship. In addition, each person involved has to be checked out thoroughly before he is approached for service. I can't tell you the number of times we have come close to blunders in that area, but somehow we have always lucked out. Everything has to be kept top secret within the group. This is vital because we doubt very seriously that the ruling regime even knows of its existence. For them to find out would spell disaster. Paul, not only do you know the way to our destination, you also have the skills needed for some of the final touches."

"What skills are those?"

"When we leave, there will be no returning; therefore, we need help calculating the supplies that must go with us. You, I believe, have readings on the environment that we will encounter. This, of course, will figure heavily into who and what we take."

"How large is this vessel?"

"Let's just say it is huge."

"How many people will be going?"

"Those details have not been worked out as of yet. Much will depend upon how long the journey takes. How long, Paul? How long will the trip take?"

"Just as your part of the plan is sketchy, so is mine. Depending on the size of the vessel and what the original intent of the ship was, it could take two to three years for arrival. Now, approximately how many people will be travelling?"

"I'd say three to five hundred people."

"Wow! You mean there's a vessel out there that will accommodate three to five hundred people for two years?"

"I told you it was big."

"It must be enormous."

"You see this ship was being built as an experiment in exploration. This vessel has everything. Food can be grown aboard the ship. There is even a section for livestock. Do you see why everything has to be done slowly and secretly? We cannot let our plan fail because of impatience."

"How did your father locate such a vessel?"

"He was very big into history, true history that is, not the made-up things they now teach as history. He found some old textbooks from the twentieth century and, after a while, became very interested in some of the old ships. After doing quite a bit of cross referencing, he learned that this particular vessel had never been launched. He then surmised the relic must be in existence somewhere. His mission became to find the vessel, and he did. He also discovered the ship had to be finished."

"What percentage of the vessel is complete?"

"I'd say about seventy percent. The actual structure, that is the nuts and bolts, is finished. It's all the details, and that is slow going."

"Okay. I'd like to see the vessel, so that I can offer my opinion as to its worthiness. If it's just a hull, we have nothing."

Reggie quickly responded. "I assure you it is more than a mere hull. It is truly magnificent. I can't give you an exact time for seeing it, but I can tell you that I will take you to it in the near future. Remember, everything has to be done in secret; therefore, nothing happens quickly.

This project could be a test of all our patience and longevity as well."

As Reggie started for the door, Paul had one other question. "How did you know about my grandmother and her documents?"

Reggie smiled. "Dad told me about her a long time ago. Your grandmother was quite well known among the various groups who opposed the elites. She didn't mind speaking her mind. Sometimes it got her in hot water, but still she stood up for the values and principles that she had grown up believing. My dad thought she was one of the bravest women he had ever met. She told him that the documents from our past must be preserved at all costs. She made it her mission to print and reprint things of importance, items she thought might benefit future generations. She found unique ways to hide and store the precious words. Paul, she was quite a legend among the crowd that grew up free. You do have the documents, don't you?"

"I do indeed."

"May I have them. I promise to keep them safe. In fact, I promise you that you'll see them again. At some point, they will prove invaluable."

Paul reluctantly retrieved the precious papers and handed them unceremoniously to Reggie. All he could say was, "What's next?"

"I'm going to leave just as I came. No one notices me. That's the way I like it. I'll return to give you a progress report from time to time. Don't get nervous. It may be as much as a year before I return. Remember: don't become discouraged. Anything as good as freedom is well worth waiting for."

Paul knew Reggie was right, but years seemed like such a long time. His hope would keep him going, and he would never lose faith. If life knocked him down, he'd punch back. He had at last a reason for hope.

Reggie slipped out the door as quietly as he had entered. Paul prayed a silent prayer for Reggie's success as well as the favorable results of other members of the group, people he had not met, people who wanted to be free as badly as did he. Paul was not a patient person, but he knew it was a quality that he would more than likely be cultivating over the next several years.

CHAPTER 12

"Hey, Dad, you look like you're a million miles away." Marsha jolted him into the present.

"Yes, I guess I was a million miles away." Marsha looked puzzled. "I was just thinking about some of the folks I've encountered through the years. Some of them were quite interesting."

"Life has never been dull, has it?" she replied as she grabbed her coat and headed for the outside.

"Oh no, and who knows, perhaps the best is yet to come." Paul felt that little encouragements might be the best way to prepare Marsha. The time was short. Paul had proven to be a very indecisive person when it came to dealing with Marsha. He had gone from taking Nat and slipping away leaving behind only a letter of explanation to taking Nat and Marsha kicking and screaming if it became necessary. He prayed for wisdom to deal with any and all circumstances when the time came.

The amen wasn't more than out of his heart until the answer arrived: "Put yourself in the middle of the pain that Marsha has experienced. See what your reaction would be."

Paul thought, *I've been remembering her pain, her experiences. Isn't it enough to remember the pain she felt when her life was turned upside down as a child?*

The answer seemed to say, "You haven't gone far enough."

I don't want to go there. It was painful for us all.

"Go there," the urging continued. "Feel her pain. Then you'll be able to at least try to counter her arguments. Then and only then..."

After Reggie's first visit with Paul in the village, life continued pretty much as before. From time to time Paul would become quite restless. Usually the uneasiness would occur immediately after a visit from Reggie. Paul always believed things should be moving at a faster pace, and Reggie always assured him that haste could be their undoing. Reggie never visited more than two or three times a year. He didn't want to draw attention to the small community in the middle of nowhere, so his visits were few and far between. Paul knew that eventually the project would be complete, but he wasn't getting any younger. Though younger than he, Reggie was aging as well. Try as he would, Paul could never get Reggie to agree to a faster pace. Paul would have to trust Reggie's judgment. Months turned into years, and still Paul had not seen the transport. This contributed a bit to his anxiety. He wanted to get a handle on just what the situation might be. Reggie kept explaining to him that he would see the vessel when the time was right. There was no reason to attract unnecessary attention until there was a real reason for a viewing. Others were doing their assignments. Everything was being done so as not to jeopardize the mission. Paul's expertise would be needed in the final stages. Paul had no choice but to accept Reggie's position and move on with life, and life at the moment consisted of rearing a teenager who believed she was already grown.

Even though Marsha was eighteen years old, Paul did not consider her ready for adulthood. Therefore, when she announced to him that Nathaniel Brook was more than the older brother of Priscilla, he was a bit shocked. It had never been unusual for Marsha to spend time at the Brooks' home. After all, the girls were best friends. They had been inseparable from the beginning. Yet, as Paul considered this proclamation, he remembered Nathaniel had been escorting Marsha home after her visits. He simply assumed that Priscilla had other things to do.

"Just how serious is this relationship?" Paul questioned Marsha.

"We plan to marry."

"You're only eighteen!"

"Well, I didn't mean we're marrying today."

Paul was relieved for the time being. "Please tell me what you do mean."

"Nathaniel has several courses to be completed at Hilltop, and I want to complete my education as well."

Paul felt life returning to his body. He had been blindsided, but it at least sounded like the kids were going to exercise good judgment.

Hilltop was little more than a few buildings put together at the top of a hill that was dense with trees and undergrowth. There were several communities that sent their college-age children there. After completing high school, all the young people who had a desire to learn things that their community could not teach studied at Hilltop. After their courses were successfully completed, they received a degree of sorts. Paul would have wished for a degree from a real university for Marsha, but that was not possible. This was their chosen life. There was no going back, not that he wanted to. Marsha had a keen mind, and she would absorb what Hilltop had to offer. Paul had been offered a job at the facility several years earlier, but he turned it down. His community and his daughter needed him worse than Hilltop. Paul was confident Hilltop was safe. He didn't believe the elites even knew about the place because no surprise visits had ever been conducted that he knew about.

"How long will it take to complete your course of study?" Paul asked his daughter.

"I should be able to finish in two years. Nathaniel thinks he can finish in one more year."

Paul figured he could hold off the marriage for at least a year. He would certainly try to get them to wait longer. For now, he could rest easier.

As time passed, Paul became quite fond of Nathaniel. He had always liked the young man. He just hadn't thought of him as a partner for Marsha. Paul, with the help of the Brooks, successfully put the young people off for two years. As the two received their degrees, their next order of business was marriage. Though the village had little to do with the outside world, they tried to keep peace with the elites by abiding by the rules laid down for the rest of the country. Nathaniel and Marsha left the confines of their world early one morning to go to the nearest town to receive permission and fill out the necessary paperwork that would declare them husband and wife. A real wedding was being planned for them in two weeks. Marsha would be wearing Susie's long white dress, and Nathaniel would be dressed in the finest the village had to offer. Priscilla would be the maid of honor, and Ned would be his son's best man. And yes, Paul would give her away. A traditional wedding that he had not seen since he was a child would be held. After their marriage, Nathaniel would farm the land using techniques he had learned at Hilltop, and Marsha would teach the younger children at the school. Life seemed to be looking up for the young couple, and for that, Paul was thankful.

As the couple left in one of the village's rickety trucks, everyone in the village gathered around and wished them well. With any kind of luck, they would return by midafternoon. Though they would be gone for such a short time, this was a special day for the two even if the real event was still two weeks away. The town to which they were travelling was only fifty miles away, and they had left early. Still, Paul was astonished when he heard the old truck lumbering up the gravel road only a few hours after they had left. He could not help but think how quickly they had completed their task. He had assumed they would take longer, perhaps even take the long way home. To be completely alone was almost an impossibility in the community. Someone was always around. Close living required a tolerance for probing eyes. It was nice, however, that the eyes never spoke. Everyone was too busy to lend themselves to minding the business of others. The nature of the village made the couple's early return seem unusual.

The roar of the truck grew louder and stopped in front of Paul's home. Before he could reach the front door, Marsha ran by him. He could tell she had been crying. New marriages could be an emotional time for some people, but that's not what this was. A knot was quickly growing in his stomach. Nathaniel stepped through the door. "What's wrong?" Paul asked in a way that suggested he might not really want to know.

"There was a problem at the office of records."

"A problem?"

"Let me talk to Resa. She may want to tell you."

Paul could only think of how he didn't want to know. To know might require action. He wasn't sure he was up to the task that might be waiting. If it was a case of hurt feelings, Nathaniel and Marsha would just have to work it out. He had vowed a long time ago that he would not interfere in their personal squabbles. From the looks of Marsha, he believed it was much more than hurt feelings. The knot in his abdomen was growing tighter. A quick mental picture was coming into focus. Marsha had looked pale. Her hair was a mess, but maybe the truck's windows had been down. There was dirt on her dress. How could that have happened? His thoughts stopped midair as Nathaniel led Marsha into the small living area. She looked so small, so weak, so vulnerable. "Dad, we didn't get permission."

"That's okay. You can do it another day," Paul said it in such a way that an observer would have thought that he was comforting a disappointed child whose favorite excursion had been postponed. He still wasn't sure he wanted to hear, but the words were starting to flow like a volcano that was in the beginning stages of spewing its lava out on the unsuspecting ground.

"There was a problem," Nathaniel continued.

"What kind of problem?"

"I'll tell him," Marsha said as she looked into Nathaniel's glazed eyes. She sat down in the chair so lightly that it made her appear to be smaller and smaller.

Paul wanted to scream at her to not disappear. Instead, all he could say was, "Tell me what?"

Marsha continued, "The man at the office of records wasn't a very nice person."

Paul wanted to say, "So what else is new?" Instead, he sat quietly, willing to give the young couple all the time they needed.

"When we arrived, there was no one there, except the man. Nathaniel parked the truck next to the flat, gray building, and we went inside. The entire office consisted of one room and a smelly toilet. We felt so lucky because we had heard about the long lines that were sometimes there. But today no one was there. The man looked up from a paper he had in front of him. He had dark, piercing eyes that looked right through us. As he glanced out the window, he informed Nathaniel the truck would have to be moved to a lot down the street because some workers were going to be in the parking area. We still didn't suspect anything unusual, not even when he suggested that I stay and get started on the paperwork." Marsha's eyes glanced down. Paul could see she was filled with regret, not guilt. She continued, "Almost as soon as the motor cranked up, the man started calling me names."

"What kind of names?"

"Think of the vilest terms of which you might refer to a woman. Dad, I don't even want to say the words. The next thing I knew he was out from behind the desk and standing behind me." Her voice was starting to get high pitched and very anxious. "He started lightly rubbing my arm and telling me what a good-looking you-know-what I was. I moved his hand and told him to stop. I tried to get to the door, but he got between me and the door." Tears were coming, but still she continued. "He pushed me to the floor. I knew I had to do something; so somehow, I'm not sure how, I managed to kick him between his legs. He stumbled backward, and I raced for the door. He had conveniently locked the door, and I couldn't unlock it. He was mad now. He came toward me with an open knife. He didn't even care that Nathaniel could return at any moment. With a great deal of relief, I heard the doorknob turn, and I called for help. Nathaniel could tell that something wasn't right and kicked the door open. The monster stopped in his tracks."

By now Marsha was sobbing uncontrollably, so Nathaniel took over. "His knife and his anger were suddenly directed toward me. It was obvious what he had been up to, and he didn't mean for us to be able to tell anyone. He lunged toward me, and somehow I grabbed his arm. He wasn't very strong, but he wouldn't release the knife. In almost an act of suicide, he turned the knife toward himself. The blade went straight through his heart, and he fell to the same floor on which moments before he had thrown Resa. He was dead. We almost panicked, but we managed to keep our wits. We knew we had to get him in the truck and get out of there. No one was going to believe our story of self-defense. I walked as calmly as

I could to the truck and drove it to the office. I carefully backed to the door. Resa cleaned the office of any blood and straightened the furniture. We then headed home. His body is in the back of the truck. No one saw us. The office was in an isolated location, and there was little traffic on the road."

Paul's heart was sinking. He was thinking. In an earlier time, they would have gone together and reported the incident to law enforcement, but now, all they had was their conscience to live by. There would be no reporting, and there would be no guilty consciences for ridding the world of an animal who had probably preyed on others. "Stay here," Paul told the couple, and he went to Ned and Susie's as fast as his legs would carry him. He immediately relayed the story to the wide-eyed parents.

Ned was the first to answer, "Things like this have happened before but not in a state capacity. We want to live in peace, but sometimes the outside world won't let us."

"Happened before?"

"Yes, since you've been here, actions of self-defense have occurred at least three times. You didn't know?"

"I never suspected a thing."

"Come with me."

Paul followed Ned. They went to the truck and climbed in. Ned drove up the hill to a narrow road that was little more than a path. After a while, the truck stopped. They got out and went to the back of the truck. All the trucks had a supply of tools, and they pulled out two shovels. "We'll bury him over there." Ned pointed to an isolated area. Paul asked no questions. This was how the group survived, and in his mind, this was the right thing to do. Upon completion, the ground was arranged in such a way that not even the most skillful eye could detect a burial had taken place. Paul suspected others were there, and he had no doubt they were deserving of their fate.

Paul and Ned made sure the truck was thoroughly clean. There would be no signs of the struggle. The young couple handed over their clothes, and the parents burned every stitch. The code of the community was, as Paul learned, the deed would never be mentioned again, and it wasn't. If anyone in the village knew, it was never mentioned. Each family understood that their time to protect a loved one might come at any time. These people were nonjudgmental. They accepted life as it came.

Two days after the event, a special meeting of the leaders of the village was held. It was decided that in the future all permits would be issued through the community. If the elites deemed the permits void, they would request a special office in which to conduct their business. To Paul's knowledge, no other village had ever had their permits voided.

Two weeks later, Nathaniel and Marsha were married. They were the first couple to receive permission by the community. The wedding was beautiful. At the close of the ceremony, scarcely a dry eye could be found in the building, and Paul was no exception. Paul was certain that the entire community knew of the events of the past weeks, but no one said a word.

CHAPTER 13

The old man paused in his thoughts of the past. From the beginning life had not been easy for Marsha, and now that she felt comfortable how could he possibly ask her to leave this zone of seeming peace to enter a very much unknown. Not to mention, the journey was not for the faint of heart. Paul would have to take Marsha's experiences and glean them. He would have to convince her of the dangers associated with staying. Surely with the events of the day, he wouldn't have much trouble with that part of his argument. The problem would be fear itself. Fear can freeze action. It throws rational thinking into obscurity. He did not want a fearful existence for Marsha and Nat. Fear was in part how the elites had controlled the masses for years. There was always a disaster just around the corner if the ruling class didn't get their way about whatever happened to be their latest whim. After a while, most rational people caught on to their game plan, but it was too late. Protest brought disappearances, late-night raids, beatings. It wasn't too long until the masses had been beaten into subjection. Now, this was the society in which they were forced to exist. Fortunately, he, Marsha, and Nat were in a small, very small oasis, and he knew it could be wiped away at any time. Time was short. The strategy that had been worked on for years was almost complete, and still, he was unsure how the details would be met by those most dear to him.

Paul had to think once again about the past. The old man remembered the life Marsha and Nathaniel shared in their early years together... It had been decided early on that the young couple would live in Paul's home. They would construct an extra room so that it would be ready when an addition arrived. The couple was happy, and this, of course, made Paul a happy man. All he had ever wanted for Marsha was happiness.

In keeping with the law of the elites, the day finally arrived that sent Nathaniel and Marsha to the makeshift reproductive clinic in the village to seek permission to become parents. As expected, the request was granted. Paul had never heard of anyone being denied. In the outside world that might not have been the case, but in this community, people were the important aspect of the equation. The neighbors in charge of the clinic could not give permission for second children, but they didn't conduct tests either. Everyone in the village was in this life together for better or worse.

Though permission was granted, months turned into years and still no pregnancy. Marsha filled her days teaching young children at the school, and Nathaniel was an asset in the farm operation of the community. He had absorbed much information at Hilltop, and he was quite busy experimenting with some of his own ideas. Nathaniel and Marsha had gladly agreed to serve as parents to the "secrets." Only twice had their services been utilized, but it worked. The elites never checked records, and they had no idea who belonged to whom. When the elites visited, the village managed to confuse them by producing documents for several families at one time. It all seemed so plausible since the visits were to be a surprise. Yet no one in the community acted in the least surprised.

Life travelled on for the childless couple as normally as could be expected for the given circumstances until that awful time in late June. How could so many life-changing events occur in such a short period of time? The weather was experiencing one of those grand times when summer hadn't fully gained total control of the thermometer. The sun beckoned everyone to the great outdoors. With an occasional breeze, the weather was picture perfect. It was a time to be appreciated, savored. Yet Paul had grown quite skeptical, even of little gifts from nature. Just as Paul had decided to venture outside and help Nathaniel at the farm center, he heard a soft peck at the door. Who could possibly be needing him? As he opened the door, he recognized the familiar face of his friend, Reggie Locke. "Come in. Come in. It's been such a long time. What brings you out here today?" Paul could only hope Reggie had good news.

"Are you up for a little trip?"

Paul's heart missed a beat. "Today?"

"Yes, it's time for you to see the project for yourself. Soon, we'll be needing your help with some facts and figures."

"Give me just a moment to gather a few things. How long will we be gone?"

"Probably four days at the most."

"I'll have to let Marsha know. She's at Susie's house. Wait here. I'll be right back."

"Take your time. There's no rush."

Paul hurriedly went to Susie's house. He climbed the steps and knocked at the door. As Susie opened the door, he could see Marsha in the kitchen. "Resa, I'm going to be away for a few days. Can you and Nathaniel hold down the fort while I'm gone?"

"Well, it might take a lot of effort, but I suppose we can. Where are you going?"

"You know my friend Reggie? He has a few things he'd like me to take a look at. He seems to think I might be able to help him."

"I'm sure you can. Too bad you're going to miss the first blackberry cobbler of the year. Susie and I are picking berries on the far side of the hill."

Paul knew exactly what that meant. Nobody baked better cobblers than Susie, and she was sharing her secrets with Marsha. He sure hated to miss the fresh berries, but he would hate even worse to miss this long-awaited trip. "Have fun. Maybe, just maybe there'll be a few left when I return. If not, I'll enjoy some good ol' blackberry jam with hot biscuits." Paul was getting hungry just thinking about the delectables. With those words, he walked over to Marsha, hugged her, and told her he'd see her in a few days.

When Paul returned to his home, Reggie was on the front step. "Ready to go?"

"Sure am. I couldn't be more ready."

Paul always wondered where Reggie got his vehicles. Every time he came, which wasn't too often, he was in a different vehicle. The fact that he had a vehicle at all was a miracle, but he always drove a variety of vehicles. None of them stood out as anything special. Still, there were so many of them. After considering how he might phrase such an inquiry, Paul blurted out, "Where do you get so many vehicles?"

"Well, let me just say that the group has access to several vehicles. We draw far less attention if we drive different vehicles. The same transport to the same place even over a period of years could easily draw unnecessary attention. So far, we've avoided that kind of attention."

Paul could tell they were travelling southwest. "How long will it take to arrive at our destination?"

"I'd say we should arrive by midnight if we don't encounter any difficulties. You did bring identification, didn't you?"

"Right here in my pocket." Paul thumped his shirt pocket.

For "elite" purposes, he was once again Gabe Lawson. They might or might not be stopped. Either way, the two didn't want to get crossed up on a technicality like who they were. Through the years Reggie Locke had remained Reggie Locke. Somehow, he had always slid under the elites' radar. When Reggie travelled, he always had a purpose that seemed to make perfect sense to the elites. Today he was taking Gabe Lawson to check on the progress of the desert mouse. Reggie had files and folders in the back of the truck that confirmed his story. There was even a machine that Reggie claimed would call the mouse to their whereabouts. No doubt it was bogus. Paul smiled at the thought of Reggie calling mice, and the elites believing the story. His smile faded as he thought, *How did we get to this point? How did an intelligent society reach the point that a group of incompetents could rule with such an iron fist?* Paul knew the answer.

Though just a child when the world fell apart, he remembered no one did anything. It was easier to let the loud voices have their way than to create ripples. Ripples nothing. Huge waves, even tsunamis should have been formed. The supposed illustrious ones should have been told in no uncertain terms to peddle their wares somewhere else. A nation that allows its smallest yet most vocal group to always have its way will soon learn why that group is small. They usually aren't the most productive in society. Soon, their squeaky wheel will not only get greased, but there will be no oil for the rest of the population. How could such a strong country have been so passive?

Reggie hit a hole in the otherwise relatively smooth road. "Sorry. They just don't make them like they used to." Paul wasn't sure if Reggie was referring to the roads or the vehicles. Either way, the same could be said of both.

It was time for a serious discussion. "How far along is the project?"

"I think you will be pleased, but we are still several years from completion."

"Look at us, Reggie. We're not getting any younger. Right now, we're in good health, but things change. If something happened to either of us, who would continue the work?"

"Rest assured the group knows of you and your whereabouts. They will find you if something happens to me. The larger issue concerns the knowledge of our destination. You still have not divulged the location of where we are going. Isn't it time?"

Paul thought his answer through before replying. "I made a deal with you years ago, and you know me well enough to know that I keep all my bargains. Reggie, trust me when I say to always remember 'The destination is always with me.'"

The rest of the trip went rather uneventful. They passed through two checkpoints, and Reggie handled the guards like a pro. He didn't miss a beat as he told the guards about the great virtues of the desert mouse. They became so interested in the mouse's story that they barely glanced at Paul's paperwork. The journey continued with Reggie and Paul swapping driving duties from time to time. The trip was long, and an occasional respite was wonderful. On the last leg of their travel, Reggie announced, "We're almost there."

Paul wondered where "there" was. They were in the middle of the desert. All Paul could see was rock formations and sand. "Where?"

"Right around this next hill and to the left."

Paul's eyes pierced the night as they rounded the corner. "Where?" Paul asked with a little sarcasm. He was looking straight up at a huge mountain.

"Right here."

"Here?"

"Surely you didn't think a project of this magnitude would be setting out in the wide open for every elite passing by to see."

"I'm not sure what I expected. Remember, I have been waiting years to see this vessel."

"I'm sorry. I should have warned you of what to expect. You see, the vessel is in the mountain."

"And how do we get into this place?"

Reggie didn't respond. Instead, he cut the lights of the vehicle. They sat in the dark for what seemed an eternity. "We'll sit a while longer. Someone could have seen our lights and might be curious. We can never be too careful."

Paul waited patiently. He could barely make out Reggie's silhouette in the darkness. As his eyes adjusted to the black space, some things came into view as Reggie said, "We can enter."

"How?" All Paul could see was a solid wall of rock covered with sand and dirt. The obvious was to go over, which their means of transportation was not about to do, or go around, which Reggie did not seem inclined to do. Paul glanced in his companion's direction just as Reggie pointed his index finger straight ahead. With that single motion, a hole in the side of the mountain opened. With the least amount of energy possible, the vehicle with its two occupants became one with the seemingly natural formation. As soon as the truck entered, the hatch closed tight. Reggie cut the motor. To anyone on the outside the place was an eminent domain for all the wildlife of the desert. That alone made Paul shudder. His mind's eye saw slithering snakes and long-fanged coyotes. Paul was sure the blackness was taking on a dimension of its own. The darkness was heavy. He had never been in a darker place. There was not even a star to offer guidance, no moon, no shadow. The mountain was black. Paul could not even hear Reggie breathing, though he was sure his friend could hear him.

After what seemed forever, Reggie said, "Twentieth-century technology. Is it great or what?"

"Huh?" By now, Paul was sweating profusely. He needed air, and he needed it fast. "What are we doing sitting in the middle of the desert inside a mountain?"

"Oh, you'll see. I'm sorry. I should have warned you of what to expect. I've been here so many times that my early fears have turned to fascination."

"What else do I need to anticipate?"

"Everything else is pretty straightforward, though quite captivating."

"Why must we sit in this darkness so long?"

"When the architects of this place were in the planning stage, secrecy was vital. They, therefore, placed safeguards that would ensure only those who were supposed to be in here would ever venture inside. You just experienced one of those defenses. You had nowhere to go. An intruder would have never entered. The fear would have been too great."

A dim light came on, and Paul saw Reggie point his index finger in the direction of the beacon. "How are you opening these doors?"

"Let's just say the ability is always with me." That was all Paul was going to learn about the invisible key for now, but just like Paul's mysterious directions, Reggie had a special secret as well. "Follow me."

Paul obeyed without question. He was more than willing to leave the dark holding area that was filled with fear. As he passed through the light-filled doorway, a beep sounded. Paul froze. He couldn't move. "Oops. I forgot to turn the identifier off. Stand still." Paul couldn't wiggle his big toe. He sure wasn't going anywhere. "The machine is registering everything about you. When it's finished, I will give it an 'okay' on you. The next time you come, it will allow you to pass without so much as a sound. The apparatus can be cut off in order to allow large groups to pass, but for now, this is another line of defense to keep unwanted visitors out."

The mechanism at last released Paul. "I'm impressed."

"Just wait until you see some of the other advanced equipment around here."

The pair travelled down a long, well-lit corridor to a large metal door. Reggie punched in a code then laid his finger on a machine. The door opened into a large elevator. "We're going to the top."

Excitement was taking hold of Paul. This was the moment he had been waiting on for years. The giant elevator moved, and the what ifs took over. What if the whole plan was just a big joke? What if the vessel was so rickety it would be impossible to make the journey? What if his calculations were wrong? What if… what if… what if? Paul commanded his thoughts to cease just as the moving room did likewise. He had never been on an elevator quite like this one, not even as a child. In fact, he had no idea such a machine existed. It was the enormity that caught his attention. At least a hundred people, maybe more, could board at one time. There were few buttons, so he knew few levels existed. Yet the mountain was huge, and he suspected that somehow it was filled to capacity. The anticipation grew as the doors of the gigantic machine inched open. Then there it was. Paul's mouth dropped open. He had never seen anything like it. He could remember seeing pictures of the great travel machines as a child, but this one was different. The ones he had seen were built for three or four people. This one was constructed for a small city. It was spectacular. Paul looked at Reggie in amazement and asked, "Will it move?"

"We hope so."

For the time being, Paul let the remark slide. He was too amazed to question the practicality of the enormous mechanism.

"Would you like to get closer? Be careful as you cross the bridge. It's a long way to the bottom."

Paul moved almost like a robot. He was in a near catatonic state. He was confused. He was not sure what he had expected, but it sure wasn't this. After a few steps, Paul regained his voice, "How was something like this made and then hidden all of these years?"

"It wasn't easy. When the socialists came into power many years ago, there were many in powerful positions who were opposed to the regime. When they realized all was forever lost, many set about to salvage what they could of a free society. Those brave souls who still clung to their hope of regaining freedom decided to erase from records any and all projects that might help the ruling class with their propaganda agenda. Many in top-secret positions risked everything to prevent the elites from gaining access to very privileged material. Many people 'disappeared' when the erasures were discovered." Paul jumped. His dad had disappeared, and he had never understood why. Perhaps after all these years, he was getting answers. "Fortunately for us, no one revealed anything." Paul thought about how his dad would have never betrayed a friend or his country. "All was kept secret, and that includes this project. The project was actually started in the late twentieth century, but budgetary restraints caused it to be mothballed. Except for a few scientists, the project was all but forgotten. Dad had heard rumors of a secret site in the desert. His knowledge of history caused him to think that the stories might possibly have substance. After Dad realized what you had found, he knew he had to try to find this place. He had connections, and finally he was able to contact a general from the old order. Dad had been assured by trusted associates that the general had a similar passion to break the fetters of the new regime. At last, this place was resurrected."

The pair moved closer and closer to the monstrosity. Paul wasn't sure that he was seeing correctly, but he was. There it was painted in vivid red, white, and blue on the side of the vessel. It had been years since he had seen one, but somehow it brought a lump to this throat. Instinctively, his right hand went to the center of his chest. G had said respect for a way of life and those who had died under that flag required a salute. He had never forgotten. "Will we be travelling under that flag?"

"We will indeed."

"Good, very good," Paul said softly as if to speak louder would have disturbed those very dead who had passed in defense of that flag. Paul stopped in his tracks and looked directly at Reggie. "We really are going to travel in space, aren't we?"

"We really are."

A long silence ensued. The words settled on the two friends. After years and years of hoping, planning, and praying, their mission in life was about to come to fruition. They were resigned to their fate whatever that might be. There was no turning back. They would plow ahead into the vast unknown. They would tackle problems no man had ever encountered, and somehow they would succeed. There was no room for failure. In fact, the word had been deleted from their vocabulary. They were evolving into fearless warriors without even realizing the change. Life circumstances had mounted one on top of the other until new creatures had emerged. These beings gave the appearance of being calloused on the outside, but their humanity was very much alive and well on the inside. They were good people looking for a life that most thought was long ago dead and buried. They now viewed themselves as keepers of the secret… man will always strive to be free. There were few exceptions. The two took a great deal of pride in searching on their own for the details of the past, and what they had discovered was that most successful civilizations had to have a free society. The people had to have the freedom to pursue all that they desired. Theirs was no different; however, to accomplish this end, they would have to leave. Much like the early settlers to the New World, they would be searching, looking for a better life. Harsh conditions might exist, but they would overcome. They had to; there would be no returning.

"Professor?"

The word jolted the two out of their world of thought. Without thinking, Paul faced the voice and immediately recognized the man. "My, how easy it is for two years to turn to twenty," Paul said.

"I wasn't sure you would remember me."

"How could I forget the man who rescued me? I even remember your name… Adam Crane. What took you so long?"

"Things never worked out to get out to your community. We've found that the least amount of travel is the best travel. At this stage, we certainly don't want any questions."

Reggie broke in, "Adam lives here. He is overseeing all the supplies that board the ship. Any adjustments that must be made must go through him."

"How close are we to completion?" Paul asked.

Reggie responded, "As you can see, the ship is almost finished. There's still a few problems to be addressed, but no major obstacles. Now the delicate matter of the passengers' needs for at least two years must be met. Everything we'll need must go with us, and much of that is in short supply. We have connections, but the process is slow."

"How long, Reggie?"

"Hopefully, five to ten years."

"Can't we go any faster?"

"Haste could bring about undesirable consequences."

Adam broke the tension. "Here's what we need from you." Adam handed Paul a list of questions that needed to be studied and calculated. There were many items on the list that a child with any math skills could have completed, but then the serious entries appeared, survival items… oxygen for X number of days for all passengers, medicine for outbreaks of deadly diseases. The list went on and on.

"I'll be glad to calculate for you, but this looks like a busy list to me."

Reggie and Adam looked at each other. Reggie answered, "I suppose it is. We wanted to keep your interest. Your value will come in the last phase of our project. Paul, you're the only one who can guide us to our destination. We have a captain and crew who are ready to go at any time, but they are nothing without your guidance.

Forgive us for insulting you, sir." Reggie politely removed the list from Paul's hand.

"There's nothing to forgive. I know what my worth is to the mission. I appreciate your confidence in me. I will not let you down; however, in ten years I will be in my mid-seventies. Is that going to be a problem?"

"In ten years, we also will be older than the usual age for such travel. We have run the figures, and according to the data, we will be fine."

"Run the figures?"

"Yes, this machine has it all."

Adam added, "There's one thing we want to ask of you."

"Just ask."

"Would you mind appearing to grow old?"

Paul laughed. "I am old. There's no appearing to be done."

"No, I mean decrepit."

"Why?"

"From time to time, you will be making trips to this place. No one would suspect a feeble old man of planning space travel. In the process, do not become feeble. Exercise, exercise, exercise. We want to keep you in tip-top shape. Don't play the role to the point that the elites want to haul you away. Just act what in another life would be your age."

Paul replied, "If that will help our mission be a success, I'm on board. Now, do you all mind if I see the inside of this… this thing?"

Before Paul could finish his sentence, the large metal door was moving upward. The movement was smooth, effortless. Everything about this machine was an amazement, so different from the antiquated workings of his existence. Before the entrance was half revealed, Paul could see the beginning of a new life. The room was bright, shiny, clean, very sterile. Ten or twelve people would easily fit into the area. Heavy metal benches were attached to the wall with huge bolts.

Reggie noticed Paul appeared to be speechless. "This is the main way in and out of the vessel. Not only does it serve as a regular entry, it is also a decompression room. It may become necessary for someone to go outside while we are en route. This could prove to be a very important sector of the ship. I think you'll be especially impressed with the next area."

Reggie pushed a button, and the door slid to what appeared to be about an eight- to ten-foot hallway that connected the decompression room to a large gathering area. As Paul stepped through the doorway, he gasped and stopped in his tracks. There on both sides of the walls of this magnificent machine hung G's documents. They were in frames that appeared to be made into the walls. Paul looked at each one carefully. The lines where G had folded them were still visible. How carefully she had done her job. It had been a lifetime ago that he had actually read the instruments. The first one was the Mayflower Compact. He touched the frame gently. A beginning. They too were going to begin anew. The Declaration of Independence was followed by the Articles of Confederation. On the opposite wall was The Constitution of the United States. How so many words could have been placed in such a small amount of space escaped him, but there it was followed by the Bill of Rights. To the left of the doorway leading to the open area was a framed

American flag. How beautiful the sight! To the right was the Pledge of Allegiance. Paul felt overwhelmed. They indeed would be traveling as Americans with all the hopes and dreams of those earliest of settlers. When a person entered the vessel, he would be immediately reminded of why he was there, and just maybe, those who had made such brave sacrifices along the way would be honored by their attempts to restore freedom. "Thank you, G."

After Paul had been given ample time to absorb the reverence of the moment, the tour continued. The large open area was a common area for meetings, socializing, and anything else that required a large space. They went from one end of the vessel to the other. They examined everything from the lower animal level to the upper control area, from the living area to the work area, and from the medical facilities to the body disposal area. Paul was impressed. For the first time, he believed his hopes could be realized. Life was going to be different.

The following morning Reggie and Paul started back to the village. Time seemed to fly. Paul couldn't contain his eagerness. He talked and talked. He was like a child who had just been told that a toy he had wanted for years had been placed on order, and it would arrive in a few days. Paul was excited. But with every tall mountain comes a deep valley, and Paul Allen was about to fall into a very low glen.

CHAPTER 14

The old man opened his eyes. He didn't want to remember. The events that followed his return home were painful. Yet, in order to convince Marsha, he would relive the hurt…

Shortly after midnight, Paul and Reggie turned into the long, gravel road leading to the village. Paul sensed something was amiss almost immediately. Suddenly, two stick-toting bodies popped out of nowhere directly in front of the truck. Reggie slammed on the brakes and halted just before making contact with the spooky figures. It was obvious the two meant business as the sound of wood and metal came together. At first, Reggie and Paul were overcome with surprise, but finally reason started to take over. Paul jumped out of the truck. "What's going on?"

No sooner did Paul speak than the young boys halted. "Mr. Lawson?"

"Yes, who did you think it was?"

"We weren't taking any chances."

"Chances?"

"A lot has happened in the past few days."

"Like what?"

"Mr. Lawson, you need to go home. No, on second thought, go to the Brooks' home."

"Why? What's going on?"

"Sir, the adults will tell you everything. We're staying here to guard the entrance."

"We've never guarded the entrance."

"Sir, just go to the Brooks' home."

Reggie and Paul jumped into the truck. They travelled as fast as they dared on the bumpy road. Neither said anything. To speak would have required speculation that neither wanted to pursue, but Paul was sure something dreadful had occurred. As the vehicle wheeled into the village, the two noticed that many homes had lights burning. This was unthinkable. Conservation was the order of the day. "Drive to the Brooks' house, Reggie."

Paul noticed eyes peeking out the windows. Reggie said nothing. Reggie seemed to know. He had seen how the powers that be operated, and usually it was not pretty. As soon as the truck slowed, Paul bailed out. He ran to the Brooks' door and beat on the entrance. In short order, Susie was looking out the corner of a curtain the way only a frightened person will do. Seeing Gabe, she immediately opened the door. Paul with Reggie on his heels entered quickly. "What's going on?"

Paul could tell Susie had been crying. "Susie, what is it? What's happened?"

Susie burst into tears. "Oh, Gabe, it's awful."

"What? Susie, are the kids okay?"

Susie was now weeping to the point that she could not speak. Paul could only place his arms around her and offer her the comfort of his presence. As Paul consoled Susie, he noticed movement out of the corner of his eye. He turned, and there stood Marsha. She was pale to the point of looking beyond this world. Her eyes were glazed like an animal without hope. She moved toward him with stiff zombie steps.

"Marsha, what's wrong? Please, please tell me."

"They're gone." Her voice was a monotone.

"Who's gone?"

"Nathaniel, Priscilla, they're all gone."

"Gone? Where?"

"Taken. Dad, they came and took them."

"Who came?"

"Agents of the elites."

"Why?"

The question appeared to have no answer. Then a woeful response, "Because they could."

Susie's tears had slowed to the point that she could speak between sobs. "Gabe, they took all the men between the ages of eighteen and thirty-five. We don't know why."

Paul was stunned. He could only look in Reggie's direction. Reggie's head was dropped as he leaned against the wall for support. Reggie felt he was witness to a moment that was meant for family only. Reggie slowly raised his head and quietly said, "This sometimes happens when the elites think a village has grown too strong. It's their way of controlling."

Susie's sobs suddenly turned to anger. "Controlling what? A few little houses in the middle of nowhere?"

Paul, willing to get to the problem at hand, said, "You said they took the men. How did Priscilla get taken?"

"We're not sure. She was the only female taken. Gabe, she'll be all right, won't she?" Desperation was in her voice. She suspected the answer as much as did he. The quiet tears rolled this time, the tears that only a mother can cry. "Gabe, they took both of my children. Why?" With each rehearsal of events the pain opened new wounds, wounds that might well take a lifetime to heal.

"Where is Ned?"

Through her sobs, she said, "He and the other men are trying to follow them. The problem is they left about an hour after the thugs. The only thing they knew was the intruders went left at the end of the gravel road."

"Reggie, let's go and see if we can gather any clues. Susie, will you and Resa be okay?"

Paul's words seemed to bring a ray of hope. Susie looked at him. For a moment the sorrow faded. "Resa, the baby, and I will be just fine."

"Baby? What baby?"

"Dad, I'm pregnant. I told Susie while we were picking berries. Dad, Nathaniel knows. That will make him try harder to come home, won't it?"

"You know if there's any way to get back here, he will. He loves you very much."

"Please find Nathaniel and Priscilla. Please find all the men."

"Everyone is doing all they can I'm sure," Paul replied. With those words, Paul and Reggie headed for the door. There was no time to let the news of Marsha's pregnancy settle in. This should have been a time of joy. Instead, sorrow ruled. "I'm not sure when we'll return, but please,

please take care of yourselves. If anyone strange comes into the village, head for the other side of the mountain. You were safe there earlier, and you'll be safe there again." Paul then turned around and headed for Marsha. He gave her a big hug and tried to reassure her that everything would be fine. He certainly did not want to convey his own misgivings.

When both men were settled in the truck, Paul broke the silence. "What's this all about?"

"It could be a number of things."

"You've been out there. Now what's going on?"

"I strongly suspect they think the village is growing too fast. They have all the slips for pregnancy permission. Yet the town probably has quite a few more people than those pieces of paper indicate. What better way to slow the population growth."

"Why just the men?"

"The men suit their purpose a little better. You see, they have forced labor camps and worse."

"Worse?"

"Paul, these men are in big trouble. These people are ruthless. They think nothing of torture, experiments. You get the picture."

"What are our chances of locating them?"

"My guess is nil."

Paul was shocked. "No chance at all?"

"These people always have a vile plan. They wouldn't just take a truckload of men without having an exact destination. We can look and look, but we won't find them. The only hope is that occasionally a few of the captives escape; however, they never return to their homes. They know better. You see, it is revealed on their journey as to what is going to happen to them. They are so terrified by what they are told that they would never put their families at risk."

"How do you know these things?"

"I've encountered some of the escapees. Paul, some of the most proficient workers in our project are former captives, and they *do* have stories to tell."

"I want to search anyway."

"We will, but don't get your hopes high."

The two then headed out into the early morning. As dawn broke, they had seen no signs of the captives or any of the rescuers for that matter. Paul was scanning the countryside. He was not ready to give up. Off in the distance, he saw what appeared to be a heap of garbage on the side of the road. As they neared, he realized it was not garbage but what was left of a person. They moved closer and closer. Paul saw the remains move. "Stop, Reggie!"

Reggie braked so quickly it threw them both forward with a jolt. Paul pushed the door open and jumped out. The creature moved once again. As Paul approached the mass, two eyes bolted open. "Please help me."

As Paul studied the two eyes with the barely audible voice, he recognized the person. "Priscilla?"

"Please help me," the creature said once again.

"You're going to be all right, Priscilla. We're here, and we're going to take you home." Paul didn't know whether to move her or let nature run its course. He removed his shirt and placed it under her head.

Reggie was moving things around in the truck in preparation for an injured passenger. "Paul, let's get her in the truck." The two carefully lifted her and put her in the cab. Paul cradled her head, while her feet were in Reggie's lap.

The two looked at each other. Paul was becoming emotional. This was the young woman who had played such an important role in his family's life. He loved her like she was his own, and just as there had been times when he could do nothing to aid his own daughter, he could not help Priscilla. The two men were witnessing the last moments of Priscilla Brook's time on this earth. She was about to be free. She would soar. She would go where no human animals could ever touch her again.

The weak voice said, "Tell Mom and Dad I love them. Take care of Resa." And almost as a postscript the faint voice added, "Nathaniel has a key." With those words, the rigid body went limp. Priscilla was dead. Tears ran down the face of Paul and dropped onto Priscilla's once beautiful hair. He gently stroked her hair as if the compassionate act might restore life to her body. This woman was more than just an in-law of the family. He had watched her grow up with Marsha. They were inseparable. He had always believed Priscilla had plotted to make sure Marsha and Nathaniel were together. She was a good, young woman. And now, she was gone, another victim of this cruel, godless regime. Oh how he hated what these people stood for.

Upon arriving at the village, Reggie and Paul took the precious remains to Paul's house. Paul then sent for the family who attended to the deceased in the community. He then left Reggie at his house to meet the group while he slowly walked to Susie's house. As he entered the house, Susie sensed bad news. "What's wrong? What's happened?"

"It's Priscilla."

"Where is she? Is she okay? Please tell me she's okay."

"I'm sorry."

Susie fell to her knees and sobbed as only a mother could weep. Paul tried to console her, but for now, it was useless. Marsha heard the commotion and came into the room. "What's wrong?"

"Priscilla's gone."

"No. She can't be." All Marsha could do was sit back in the chair and stare into space while tears flowed effortlessly down her face.

Paul did his best to take care of the two women. He was thankful that Reggie was there so that Susie did not have to see Priscilla's ragged body. Reggie took care of all the early details. Later that day, the older men returned empty-handed. No young men. No Nathaniel. No clues.

Paul was given the task of breaking the news to Ned. He too was overcome with grief. Such pain, such misery, and just when Paul thought he could take no more, he thought of the grandchild who was on its way. The thought of the child brought fresh hope. Paul became all the more determined that the child would not grow up in this world. The matter was sealed. It was a fact. The child was not about to experience a life where his existence hinged on the whims of the elites. His grandchild was going to be raised free. Of this, he was sure.

When Reggie left the following day, Paul thanked him for being there, but even with all the sorrow, Paul called him aside. "Please rush the project."

"Paul, we're doing our best."

"I know you are, but Reggie, I don't want my grandchild growing up in this world."

"Neither do I."

"What do you think Priscilla meant about Nathaniel having a key?"

"I'm not sure. Perhaps she was delirious. We may never know." They shook hands and parted. It would be quite a while before they saw each other again, and life continued.

CHAPTER 15

The old man paused in his thoughts. There was no need to dwell on the past at this time. The ship was ready. Though he had not seen Reggie in a while, he had a feeling that would not go away. He was sure, very sure that the vessel was ready for its passengers. They were probably waiting for just the right time to begin the gathering in of those making the long journey. Paul's recollections had cleared his thinking. He was ashamed as he thought about how he had considered dividing the family. He realized that Marsha must have a say in their decision. With the recent events, Marsha would have to be told that they would be leaving soon. She had always been comfortable in the little village and had never shown any inclination toward wanting to leave. Somehow Marsha had made peace with her life. But now she would have to abandon the familiar. She might refuse to leave, but he could never leave her behind. The family was not going to be

separated. The thugs would return, and they would mean business. He had relived her pain. Now, how much did he reveal of his own pain? It was his hope that he would be able to explain the mission and she would eagerly agree to leave this existence. Somehow he didn't believe that was likely. How much would he reveal? To tell her everything, he would have to open wounds that had long been closed, never healed just closed. What would it do to him when doors opened that had long ago been closed, not locked just closed. To relive the pain and horror might be more than this seventy-five-year-old man could stand. He would have to risk all and reveal horrors stacked in the back of his mind, things that had not been thought on in years. Paul took pride in looking back to gain momentum for the future. Now, he would look back with the hope that the past would thrust him and his family to the future. Still, how much did he reveal? In order to convince Marsha that they must leave, he would have to tell her all the shocking stories that he could remember. Their very existence depended on his truthfulness. He couldn't mince words. All must be told. Marsha's timing was perfect. She entered the house and slowly removed her coat.

"Hey, Dad, what's on your mind? Your expression looks like you were far from here."

"Oh, I was very far from here."

"Past or future?"

"Both," the old man said without changing his expression.

"I don't understand."

"Can we have a serious talk?"

"Look, Dad, I know those thugs arriving didn't do anything for either of us, but you took care of it. We're still here, right?"

"They'll return. It will be a while, but they'll be back. Just as soon as they think they don't risk contamination, we'll see them again."

"Maybe they'll just forget about us and mark us off their list."

"You're kidding, right? They don't forget evil. They might not remember how to spell their names, but they don't forget to inflict pain and suffering."

"I know you're right. Yet I don't know anything we can do but sit tight and pray."

"What if you could put feet to those prayers?"

"What are you talking about?"

"What if we could leave, start over, give Nat a new life?"

"Impossible."

"Not much faith in your prayers, huh?"

"I have faith to believe God will see us through this life. Look how far we've come."

"And how far is that?"

"We're still here. We're alive."

"Yes, and we flinch at the sound of any vehicle coming into the area. We're not secure."

"Is anybody?"

Paul took a deep breath. "What if we could be? I'm serious. What if we could be?"

"I don't know."

"You don't know? How could you not know! Your husband was physically removed from your life, your best friend was murdered, your in-laws have been devastated for years, and you don't know. When do you think they'll come for Nat?"

"He's just a little boy."

"So was I."

"But that was different."

"How?"

"The regime had just come into power when you were removed from your home. They were looking for the best and the brightest. They see nothing special in Nat. We make sure of that. Besides, they think you and your family perished long ago."

"What if they need children for experiments. Where do you think they'd get the subjects?"

Marsha's face grew pale. "Well, I suppose they'd go to orphanages and families deemed worthless."

"My dear, how do you think they view us and other villages like ours? Worthless, good for nothing."

Marsha sat down in a chair close to her dad. She knew he was speaking the truth, but she had dismissed thoughts of this nature from her mind. After all, her entire life had been comprised of accepting whatever came her way be it good or bad. She had learned to not question. She just bore whatever burden was placed on her. This made her resolve strong, though gentle. "Dad, I can't leave," she said with the softest voice possible.

"What if I offered you the chance to experience freedom, none of this business of moving to another village? I'm talking about real freedom."

"I'd say there's not a place like that on the face of the earth."

"You would be correct."

Her head bolted from its bowed position. "What are you talking about?"

"Marsha, the things I'm about to say to you will sound absurd, but trust me. The words are true. We have the opportunity to travel to a distant world."

"What? That's impossible. Space travel was abandoned long ago in favor of this utopia."

"Not exactly. Several projects were mothballed. When this low-life regime came into power, some people in high places decided to erase certain projects from files. The elites were more interested in staying in power than questioning such matters. Space travel was low on their list of priorities, but others saw it as a way of escaping. Did you never suspect that my absences with Reggie were more than a ride through the country?"

"I always accepted what you said."

"Then please believe me when I say that our journey is possible. Marsha, I've seen everything."

"Everything?"

"Yes, I've seen the vessel that we'll maneuver through space, but just as importantly, I've seen the planet that we'll be travelling to. From all of our readings, it's a place very much like earth, but for some reason, it is not inhabited. Perhaps it was created just for us."

As the conversation settled on her, Marsha jumped to her feet. "This is ridiculous. Did you think I would fall for such a prank? I'm shocked at you. Yes, I'm somewhat gullible but not stupid."

"Marsha, it's true. I'm not kidding! I'm as serious as I can be. In a few days we'll need to leave."

"I'm not going anywhere, and neither is Nat."

"Marsha, be reasonable. There is no future here."

"And you think there is a future in planet hopping? What am I saying? This is lunacy. Have you considered the possibility that this scheme might fail? This is an untested and untried endeavor."

"I know. I know, but the best minds from before the regime took over believed it would work."

"And where are these best minds?"

"Most are dead, but their knowledge was conveyed to the next generation. I'm one of the few that's left. Marsha, I'm an old man, and I want to feel freedom once more before I die. You and Nat have never tasted freedom. I want this for you two more than I can say."

"You are serious about this, aren't you?"

"Yes."

"Dad, how are you going to make such a journey? You can barely walk."

Paul jumped out of his chair and performed a little jig that would have made any Irishman proud. Marsha's mouth dropped open. "I'm as good physically as I was thirty years ago. My infirmities are all part of the ruse to throw the elites off. No one would ever suspect a feeble, old man of being involved in such a mission. I'm fit for the journey."

"Dad, I can see you're serious, but Nat and I will not be going."

"Marsha, please think about it."

"There's no need. There's nothing to think about."

"Why?"

"Dad, what if he returned, and we weren't here?"

"Who?"

"Nathaniel, of course."

"Oh, Marsha. No, darling, he isn't coming home."

"He could. You don't know."

"You don't know these people."

"And you do?"

"I've dealt with these people since the takeover. Marsha, if Nathaniel was alive—which I seriously doubt—he wouldn't come home. He wouldn't put you and Nat in harm's way. He loved you too much for that. These people are ruthless. They'll stop at nothing. Maybe it's time you heard a little more of what these people are capable of."

Before Marsha could speak, Paul's brain was framing the stories that Marsha was going to hear. He didn't want to leave out anything. The smallest detail might sway her. He had not wanted to tell these stories. It was easier to talk about the good times on the farm, but hideous, unspeakable things had occurred there as well. Those were laid in the far recesses of his mind, but he felt them moving to the front. He knew they were about to spill out in the form of mean, ugly words. He didn't want to talk about those things. It was easier to remember the beautiful stories, but he was desperate. He would try to make the events matter-of-factly. He would try to stay detached. That way he might be able to keep emotions at bay. He looked Marsha straight in the eyes.

"You've heard me tell Nat many of the good stories about my early childhood. Now, let me tell you how my childhood ended." The old man paused. A distant look came over his face. He was almost assuming another personality.

"You don't have to do this."

"Oh yes I do. I want you to know these creatures. I want you to be able to truly want this existence for yourself and Nat."

"I've always known your acceptance of this regime was difficult."

"Difficult? Intolerable! I hate everything the elites support, and you should as well."

"I do, but I'm not able to change anything. This is the life that I was born into."

"But you can change that life."

"What am I swapping this for? Can you truthfully tell me this new existence will be better than what we now have?"

"I can tell you that any successful civilization has to work hard to maintain its values, or it loses the right to exist. The previous generation became lazy and lost that right, but we've got a second chance."

"No, Dad. The chance is yours, not mine and Nat's."

"Listen to me. Do you know how I came to be removed from my parents' home?"

Marsha shook her head.

"Well, let me tell you. I remember it like it happened yesterday. I wish the memory wasn't so vivid. I was just a child, about Nat's age. The regime had taken control of the country. In the beginning they tried to make everyday life appear normal, but it wasn't. I was still attending the state public school. It was announced at school that tests would be administered the following day to determine what skills we had. After all, we would certainly want to fill our role as a contributor to this flawless society. When I arrived home, I told Mom about the tests. I noticed that her usual cheerful self suddenly turned all serious. She explained to me that I must do poorly on the tests. This was coming from a woman who demanded excellence. I was sure she was confused. There was no way I was going to deliberately miss the answers to those questions. And in my childlike wisdom, I didn't.

"Several weeks later, the facilitator sent a note home to Mom explaining that I had been chosen to attend a special school where there were other children like me. With my intelligence, they were sure I would someday be an elite. What they really meant was that someday I would be used by the elites to maintain their control. When Mom read the note, she almost fainted. The note gave an address where parents could go if they had questions. The very next day Mom and Dad headed for the location on the note. They had decided I wouldn't attend school that day. Instead, I would stay with Pops and G.

"Mom and Dad had heard that children were usually picked up at school the following day after a note was sent home. The state claimed it made it easier for the family to separate. No ugly scenes. When the state abductors arrived at school, the facilitator told them I wasn't there. However, she couldn't tell them fast enough where I lived and that my grandparents were next door if they didn't find me at home. Immediately, they went to my home, and of course no one was there. G and I were in the parlor of the large antebellum home when she noticed a vehicle coming up the long driveway. At first she wondered just who was visiting today, but as it got closer, she realized it was a state vehicle. She sent me out the back door and told me to find Pops at the barn and stay there. I no sooner went out the back door than a strange man grabbed me and threw me over his shoulder. Where he came from, I still don't know. G heard me scream and immediately tried to come to my rescue. She ordered the man to put me down. When he didn't, she fought him like a man. Her fists were doubled, and she smacked him so hard in the head that he had no choice but to release me. I started to run while she tried to finish the job, but the vehicle arrived. Two men jumped out. One grabbed me, and the other one pulled G off the other man. By this time, G was worn out. The man's liberator smacked G on the face. He then threw her to the ground and started kicking her. I struggled hard to free myself so that I could help her. Suddenly, the screaming stopped.

"A lone shot split the air, and the coward fell dead. I turned, and there stood Pops with his gun aimed at the others. The abductors were ordered to put me down and leave. Before I could be released, another boom filled the air. I screamed 'No!' as Pops fell like a mighty oak to the ground. He was gone, and I knew it. G crawled to his side, and the cowards kicked her over and over. She finally lay still, and the attack stopped. They grabbed their dead, put him in the trunk, and threw me in the back seat. I was terrified. I was crying. I was begging, pleading to stay. I was ignored. As I looked out the back glass, I saw G raise her head. I knew she would survive. G's condition looked a lot like Priscilla's except G survived. Of course, they thought she was dead. Marsha, G needed me, and I could do nothing. The animals didn't care. Havoc was their game. Marsha, I saw my own grandfather murdered like a common criminal for protecting his family. My grandmother was beaten and left for dead. Do you want this for Nat?"

"No."

"We have a chance to change things, Marsha. It won't be easy, but we're strong. We can do this. It would make Pops and G so proud to know that we have this unique opportunity to better ourselves."

"How do you know they wouldn't think we were fools?"

"Because G wanted her family to have a better life."

"Better means different things to all people."

"G always meant what she said."

"There is no way G would have encouraged such a journey."

"Don't be so sure. After I was abducted, the state would allow home visits one weekend a month. When the visits rolled around, Mom and Dad would hide G so that the elites would assume she was dead. After they left, G would come out of hiding. Mom and G would immediately begin deprogramming me. Their task was not difficult because I didn't fall for much of what the facilitators had to say unless it was part of numbers. Their other rhetoric went right past me especially since I had seen their wickedness firsthand. Since the reeducation process was quite easy, I had time to spend with my family. G and I had long talks about what had happened, and she went to great lengths to make sure I didn't blame myself for Pops's death. She could say what she would, but there was no one to blame except me. All I had to do was score poorly on that test, and the whole crime would have been averted. Still, I went along with her pleas to try to move on. On one visit, G and I were on the back porch after dark. The stars sparkled so brightly one could almost reach out and touch them. Out of nowhere she took my hands and looked me straight in the eyes and said, 'One day opportunity will present itself to you to be free. Don't hesitate. Take it.' She released my hands and pointed toward the heavens. 'Who knows, it might be a journey to another world. I can think of nothing that would make me prouder than to have descendants on such a noble expedition.' The matter was never discussed again, but she certainly left her impression on me."

"How could she have known?"

"I don't think she did. You have to remember she was from the age group that saw a man walk on the moon. To them, the possibilities were limitless. Then, crash. Their world fell apart."

"How sad."

"No, how irresponsible. How could something so powerful as freedom be allowed to slide through their fingertips? And yet, you, Marsha, have a golden opportunity that you are refusing to take. How sad, irresponsible, or anything else you want to call it can that be?"

"I'm not sure what to say," Marsha replied meekly. "It's not that I don't want a better life. I just don't seem to be able to shake off the old life, the life that included Nathaniel."

"Marsha, I don't know what to say or how to convince you."

"Perhaps you can't." She paused for just a moment. "Dad, if you were not absolutely sure Mom was gone, would you consider leaving?"

At that moment Paul looked old, very old. Renee's face flashed through his mind's eye. Leave would have never been an option. All he could say was, "Our experiences are so different."

"Maybe, maybe not. I cannot leave until I know Nathaniel's dead."

"I don't believe we'll ever know for sure. We never knew what happened to Dad. It was only about five years ago that I found out what happened to G." Paul's voice trailed off as painful memories were dredged.

"Tell me, Dad. Tell me what you remember."

"I had come home one weekend from the institution. As usual, I thought G had been hidden. Instead, Mom was given the task of telling me that G had left. I started to cry uncontrollably. Once again, my world was falling apart. Mom did her best to console me. After I settled down, Mom explained to me that G had no choice. Someone had reported to the elites that an extra person was living in our home. How anyone could have known is still a mystery. The elites showed up unannounced one day. Fortunately, G was on the back side of the farm. They tore the house apart looking for the lady they thought was dead anyway. After the episode, Mom and Dad contacted a group that accepted G. She was placed in the Freedom Underground, where she was an advocate for personal liberty the remainder of her life. Mom gave me time to let the news settle on me. Later, she led me to G's room and lovingly picked up the large family Bible. 'G said to give this to you.' I touched the Bible carefully. It was all I had left of G. Mom then explained how the cover had a secret pocket. She showed me how it worked. She told me that I must never reveal how the pocket opens or anything about its contents. You know, Marsha, this is when G became a force in the journey that's being planned."

"What do you mean?"

"I didn't realize for years how important G was. Reggie explained to me years ago how she fostered the vision for a new America, if not here then somewhere else. She became quite vocal. According to Reggie's Dad, she was a dynamic powerhouse. She knew how to move and inspire.

The elites finally figured out the strong-willed woman they had left for dead was actually alive and creating a stir in some areas of their domain. This time it was impossible to hide her. One day as she was on her way to a rally, they grabbed her right off the street. Not a soul came to her rescue. The word Mom and I later received was that she had passed away in a community home for the aged. In other words: euthanized."

"Was that not the case?"

"Reggie tells quite a different story. I never questioned her death. The system rids itself of the aged in 'humane' ways. I always thought she died a forced death, but I also assumed that her death was carried out mercifully."

"Not so?"

"Oh so very not so. Reggie says they hauled her off to an interrogation facility where they have ways of extracting the truth. The interrogators demanded to know the names of everyone involved in her underground world. She refused to tell them anything. This angered them to no end. Marsha, they hung her upside down by her ankles. She was an elderly lady. She was old enough to have been their grandmother, and still they didn't have an ounce of compassion. They cut her down just before she was about to go unconscious. They threw water in her face to revive her. No doubt they were confident she would tell all, but she refused. They then tied her to a metal table. When she refused to answer their questions, they shocked her. Finally, she collapsed. They left her for the night on that cold, metal table. The following day the ordeal started over. Their patience was growing thin. When they realized that she was not going to yield, they did the ultimate."

"Dad, we don't have to go there."

"Oh yes we do. I want you to know the sacrifice others made so that we could have this opportunity. I want you to know the life you are choosing for your son by refusing to leave. Marsha, they cut her tongue out. When she started choking, they laughed and walked away. She strangled to death on her own blood." Paul was crying at the thought that anyone could do that to his precious G. The story seemed so much worse when he told it. Paul had spared Marsha many of the gory details. He didn't tell her the process they used to extract her tongue. He didn't tell her how G had remained conscious throughout the whole ordeal. He had spared Marsha many of the details, and he knew he had done the right thing even though his account was not nearly as persuasive as the details of the execution might have been. Who knows? Perhaps Reggie had been even gentler as he related the events. Perhaps Paul had stored the images so far back they would never be recovered. Maybe Paul had tried to forget so that he could avoid grieving for G. Possibly after all these years, he was finally realizing the impact of her actions. Yes, he was sorry that she had experienced such unspeakable atrocities, but he was proud G's blood ran through his veins. She had died a patriotic American, and when his time came, he, too, would die an American.

Marsha allowed Paul to get control of himself before she said anything. Finally, she spoke. "Dad, you know what happened to G. I don't know what happened to Nathaniel."

"I know you don't. Let me tell you what happens to the elderly and anyone else who gets in the elites' way. They get sent to termination centers. I've seen one of those places, Marsha." His mind's eye saw the frightened face of the old man he had seen as a young person. The poor man was put down like a sick animal. Paul visibly shuddered. He stopped and looked at his daughter. "I never knew what happened to my dad. Sometimes we just accept and move on."

"It's been almost eleven years, and I haven't moved on. I've tried, but I still have that hope that Nathaniel is alive."

"Why would you think that? You know how ruthless these people are."

"Do you remember what Priscilla told you?"

Paul thought and thought, and it finally came to him. "Marsha, no. She was delirious."

"Yes, Dad. Priscilla said that Nathaniel had a key. If opportunity presented itself, Nathaniel escaped. I believe he's out there somewhere. He can't come back here, but I can't leave him either. My being here could be what keeps him alive. I can't abandon him."

"Just like my dad, Nathaniel's not coming back. Mom waited and hoped for years that somehow Dad would return, but it didn't happen."

"Their departures were different."

"Different people. Same reasons."

"Not exactly, Dad."

"Oh, yes. The reasons for both removals were to create havoc. That's what they do best."

"Yes, I agree, but they specifically targeted Granddad. Nathaniel was one of a group."

"I see what you're saying, but gone is still gone."

Paul quickly remembered that Saturday night many years earlier. "I recall Dad's disappearance very clearly. G had left after the fruitless search. The thugs couldn't accept defeat. Since they didn't retrieve G, they took the next best thing: Dad. The car was heard coming down the long drive, but there was nowhere to go. When the vehicle stopped, three men jumped out and ran to the front porch. They kicked in the door and ran upstairs to my parents' bedroom. Without saying a word, they grabbed Dad and left. Mom and Dad barely had time to touch hands. We never saw him again." Paul's mind stopped. He wouldn't allow himself to feel the terror he had experienced that night. The grief over his dad's departure would have to stay locked away.

"Marsha, I don't know how many ways to say this: 'Nathaniel's not coming home.'"

"You may be right, but if I quit hoping, what do I have?"

Until recently, hope was an almost forgotten virtue in Paul's world. Everything had always been very matter-of-fact. What was to be would be. This didn't leave a lot of room for hope. Paul couldn't respond to her statement of hope, so he simply moved to his next argument. "What about Nat? Don't you want better for him? Don't you think Nathaniel would want better for his son?"

"Of course he would."

"What are you going to do when they bring a truck and load up all the children? They've been known to do that you know."

"They do that to irresponsible communities."

"Says who?"

Marsha was unable to reply. She had no way of knowing if a village took care of its children or not. She certainly did not trust the word of the elites.

Paul continued. "Don't you want him to run, play, and become the free man God intended?"

"Yes, but at this point, I'm not sure anymore what that would be."

"You're proving my point. There's got to be a better existence out there. I want Nat to experience the things children are supposed to experience. I want him to have pets if he wants one without someone saying he can't."

"Dad, is that what this is all about?"

"What do you mean?"

"You want Nat to have all the things you had in your early childhood."

"Is that so bad?"

"Well, no, unless it clouds your perspective."

Paul felt his blood pressure rise. He could feel his face get hot. He was angry. "How can you possibly say such a thing? Clouds my perspective! Let me tell you, young lady, what clouds my perspective. The cruelty of this governing class 'clouds my perspective.' I don't want you or Nat to be influenced by them in any way except to realize that you don't want to be like them."

"I'm sorry, Dad. That was a poor choice of words."

"Yes, it was, but let me tell you what sealed those clouds in place for me."

"You don't have to."

"Oh yes, I believe I do. Perhaps it's as much for me as for you and Nat."

Marsha sat still as Paul began his account. "I've already told you what happened to G, and you know how Dad disappeared. That was more than enough for a little boy to handle. Through all of those upheavals, I was still expected to function at the institution as if nothing had happened. As you might guess, this was next to impossible. I had one close friend at the institution, Carnady Robbins. Carney, as we called him, was experiencing some pretty bad things as well. At night we would sit and talk about our lives back home. We didn't dwell on the bad things. Instead we focused on our pets. We both had dogs, and we couldn't wait to tell each other about our latest exploits with our beloved canine. We had no idea that a snitch lived in our dorm. We didn't realize that everything we said was promptly reported to the head facilitator. Not that it mattered, except that if a student stepped out of line, they then knew how to get to them in the most effective way.

"One day in class, our facilitator, Mrs. Snakedem, announced out of nowhere that God did not exist. I promptly raised my hand and was recognized. I insisted in my childlike way that God was real indeed. Our discussion went back and forth to the point that she grew weary and decided that I should be written up for disagreeing with the official policy of the state. To me it seemed to be no big deal, but I was wrong. The following weekend was home visitation. I so looked forward to those times. Even though G and Dad were gone, Mom made every effort to try to cushion the hard times. As usual, two armed men delivered me to my home and let me out. I thought it strange that they too were getting out of the van. The larger of the two men followed me to the sidewalk and asked if I had a dog. Of course I answered in the affirmative and started talking a mile a minute about what a great dog the Beast was. My talking must have roused the precious dog, and she poked her head around the side of the house. When she saw me, she barreled toward me. I held out my arms for her to jump on me. She leaped, and I caught her. Her big, trusting eyes said she was glad to see me. I looked up as the man lowered his gun toward the Beast. All at once, a piercing crack sliced the air. The Beast fell limp in my small arms. I screamed as blood and fragments splattered my face, hands, and clothes. Blood oozed from the dead body of the best dog in the world. The big man grabbed me by the collar. His words still reverberate in my head. 'Don't ever forget God doesn't exist.' At the same time Mom burst through the door, the man turned on his heels, and the two men left. I fell to my knees and held the lifeless body of the Beast. I cried until there were no more tears. Mom tried to comfort me, but she too was mourning. Mom and I buried her beside the barn. Marsha, the Beast trusted me to take care of her, and I failed."

"Dad, how do you figure you failed?"

"Marsha, I thought they were really interested in my dog. Funny how your perspective becomes cloudy. I knew better, especially with all the cruelty I'd seen these people administer. I let my guard down, and they killed the Beast. These were people of the same breed that had killed Pops and left G for dead. These same agents of the elites had taken Dad in the cover of darkness, and now they had murdered my dog. As a child, a growing hatred for what these people stood for was spawned. It's still there, Marsha. It's still there."

"At least you still had Grandmother."

"Yes, she lived for me. I knew she grieved for the losses in her life, but she always remained strong. After I went away to an upper division school, I was unable to come home on a regular basis. Mom lost a lot of her resolve. After a while her health started to deteriorate. She was unable to get immediate health care, and when she finally got to see a doctor, it was too late. She died a short time later. I still miss her encouraging words. She always seemed to know what to do." Paul paused. "I don't want to leave without you and Nat. What are we going to do?"

"Dad, it's been a long day. You've told me things I never dreamed possible. You've also revealed atrocities beyond comprehension. Let's sleep on our discussion. Sometimes problems fade in the sunlight."

"I don't believe either of us is going to change our minds no matter how much we sleep. Here's one other thought: Let Nat decide."

Marsha cringed. "I don't know. He's awfully young to make such a life-altering decision."

"But it is his life. Shouldn't he have a say?"

"When will you be leaving?"

"Soon. I don't know exactly when, but I know the project is almost complete."

"Let's not mention this to him or anyone else until we can be a little more specific. Perhaps he'll be enough older that he can choose a little more wisely than he would now."

"Agreed."

Just as the word popped out, Nat came through the front door. Both Paul and Marsha turned their attention straight at him. Nat threw his arms in the air. "What?" The two chuckled, breaking the tension at least for the moment. But Paul knew choices and decisions were right around the corner. He had told Nat all those wonderful stories of long ago. Surely Nat would not reject the possibility of experiencing some of the same things. Yet leaving his mother behind might be even worse. No, Nat did not need to make such choices. Somehow, though he was unsure how, Paul was going to make sure Nat would not be placed in that situation.

Paul suddenly felt tired. Today had been an exhausting day. Many memories, mostly painful, had surfaced. He had relived his life in one fast-moving day. The thugs' appearance added to his fatigue, and now Marsha's resolve to stay behind was overwhelming. Paul headed toward his bed. He pulled back the covers and crawled between the sheets. His eyes immediately closed, and sleep came. However, it wasn't the slumber of peace. The bad dreams came with horrific force. Paul heard himself scream. He jumped to attention. All the memories that were buried in the far recesses of his mind were now clattering through his head. Somehow he would entomb them once again. He sat on the side of the bed in the dark for a long while. He thought on the good things of life, his blessings. When he believed his mind to be sufficiently clear, he laid his head on the pillow. Once again, his eyes closed. This time all was calm, and he rested.

CHAPTER 16

The following morning the sun rose bright and clear. It was not quite as cool as it had been. However, with no heat, it still felt very cold. Over the years, Paul had learned to dress quite fast in the cold. He moved toward the kitchen, where his eyes met Marsha's. She said, "I haven't changed my mind."

"Didn't think you had," was the only reply Paul could manage to utter.

Nat joined the two for breakfast. "Why's everyone so quiet?"

Paul smiled. "I guess we don't have much to say."

"Not everyone's a motor mouth."

"Mom, why does it always have to be so cold in here?"

"Now, sweetie, you know we conserve our fuel for the really cold months ahead."

"This seems awfully cold to me. Gramps, when you were my age, did you freeze like this?"

A far-off look appeared on Paul's face. "Nope. We stayed cool in the summer and warm in the winter. It was just one of those things everyone took for granted. The closest we ever came to discomfort was the winter an ice storm hit. The electrical lines snapped like a tight rubber band. It took weeks to restore the power."

"What did you do?"

"Pops, Dad, and I just went to the back side of the farm where they had cleared some trees the year before. We cut the wood and brought it to the house. A fire was started in the fireplace, and we stayed warm. G even cooked over the fire. We managed just fine."

"Mom, reckon we could go ahead and start a fire in the fireplace?"

"It's a little early in the season for that. I think the community would frown on our actions."

Paul sat quietly. He didn't just think; he knew the community would be unhappy with such waste. As much as he loved these people, there was no real freedom here. In order to live here, rules of the state had to be obeyed. No unnecessary attention was drawn to the village as long as everyone complied. Therefore, regulations were strictly enforced. As badly as he hated to admit it, their tiny society was socialist in nature. Little room was left for individualism, which was how it had to be for survival. Paul had understood that from the beginning, and he accepted it. But now a chance for a better life was close, and he was unable to make Marsha see reason.

"Gramps, what are you up to today?"

"Oh, I don't know. I think my first order of business will be to take a nice, long walk." Paul rose from his chair and headed for the door as he grabbed his cane, which he certainly did not need.

"Either of you want to join me?"

"No thanks," they both said.

"We're going to Susie's to finish some quilting we started back in the summer. Nat is going to help."

Nat made a terrible frown when his mother wasn't looking.

Paul smiled as he went out the door. "Maybe next time."

Paul had a lot to think about as he turned and headed down the gravel road that led to the entrance to their existence. Paul had barely turned the first corner when he heard a vehicle's motor. Someone was slowly making his way down the bumpy road. It was best to exercise caution on their road if you wanted your transportation to survive. Paul halted and waited for the sound of the motor to come to him. Caution was his best ally as well. As the clatter and thumping of the tires rounded the corner, Paul could see a gray utility vehicle headed his way. He was quite sure the occupant had not seen him as he moved farther into the tree line. As the machine passed before his eyes, he tapped the side of the vehicle with his cane. "What are you doing here?" he demanded to know.

The startled driver halted. He baled out of his machine in a very menacing fashion. Paul started across the gravels in front of the vehicle as the occupant screamed, "What's wrong with you?"

The two men kept moving toward each other as if a battle of great proportion was about to ensue. Just before pain was expected to be inflicted, the two men warmly embraced each other. "Reggie, my friend, where have you been?"

"Out and about. Taking care of business."

"And what business might that be?"

"I don't have to tell you."

"No, I guess you don't." The conversation went from jovial to serious rather quickly.

"Hop in. We'll ease this truck to your house."

"Sounds good to me." Paul didn't say another word until they were inside the walls of his sanctuary. "Marsha and Nat have gone to Susie's for the day, so we can freely discuss our project. I wish it were warmer in here, but this is the best I can offer."

"Maybe I can offer better."

"What do you mean?"

"We're ready to launch."

Paul was stunned. Even though he had told Marsha that the time was soon, he was still shocked. "You mean ready as in today, not next year or the next? Today?"

A smile beamed across Paul's face, but it quickly faded. "What's wrong, Paul? I expected you to be turning somersaults by now."

"I want to, but I've hit a few snags."

"What kind of snags?"

"The kind that breaks your heart."

"Oh."

"Which snag do you want to hear about first?"

"I don't guess it really matters. We'll overcome each one as you present it."

"Okay, here goes. Reggie, the community is in grave danger."

"The community has always been in grave danger. All the small villages scattered around the country are in danger."

"No, this time there's a specific threat."

"What's happened?"

"Yesterday a truck pulled up and loaded the men. I just happened to be around and was gutsy enough to approach the thugs. Reggie, I told them the village was infected with smallpox."

"What?"

"It was the only story I could come up with fast enough."

"How many people live here now?"

"Maybe a hundred people. It's quite small, very self-sufficient, but very few in number. The elites mean to keep it that way. That's why they take the able-bodied men from time to time."

"How's the health of the population?"

"Quite good. We have a lady who treats us with herbs if we need medicine. She's very good at her trade."

"What age range does the population hold?"

"We have two babies all the way up to me. I'm the oldest. Ned's not far behind me."

"Ned?"

"Nathaniel and Priscilla's dad."

"Yes, I remember."

"What are you thinking?"

"Paul, we could take some of them with us. Do you think they'd be interested?"

"At this point, I don't know what to think. I just know I have to provide a way for them to dodge the coming problem. Those thugs will return, and with the lie I told, they'll burn everything in the village to the ground."

"They certainly will. It will probably be the early spring before they return, but who knows."

"Do you have any other suggestions?"

"I think we could relocate them."

"How? To where?"

"We have a whole village making the journey with us. There's only about thirty of them, but they have left. Your group could move into their town without being noticed. The place is only about twenty miles from here. At first, everything would be a little cramped, but it could work."

"What about giving them a choice?"

"Choice?"

"Yes, they could go with us or move to the village."

"That would be placing the burden of the decision on them, which is where it needs to be. The problem is we can't divulge where we're going or anything about the project."

"Reggie, can you spend the night here?"

"Yes."

"Let me have a talk with the village leaders. Everything will be presented to them in general terms, and they can decide for themselves."

"Sounds good, but remember nothing can be mentioned about our destination or how we'll be getting there. So far, everything is top secret, and that's how it must stay. Now, what's your next snag?"

"My next snag is Marsha. Your 'top secret' assumption is blown. She knows and refuses to go. I've given her argument after argument, and still she refuses."

"I rather expected you to tell her at some point. She won't tell, will she?"

"Of course not. She keeps her thoughts to herself."

"Why is she refusing?"

"She believes Nathaniel might still be alive. She believes to leave would be abandoning him."

The room grew quiet. Reggie didn't know where to begin. "Paul, I have a confession. I hope you'll be able to forgive me in time."

Paul looked confused. "What are you talking about?"

"We've known each other a long time. Have I ever lied to you?"

Paul thought reflectively. "I don't think so."

"Even when the possible seemed impossible, I didn't lie. I answered all your questions as straightforward as I could, didn't I?"

"Where's this going?"

"Paul, I just haven't always told you everything."

"What do you mean?"

"To those of us who have known about this project, it has consumed our lives, and that includes you, right?"

"Yes, I suppose so."

"The mission had to come above everything else."

"But not to the point of becoming like the elites."

"No, never."

"I'm relieved."

"But sacrifices had to be made. Some things we willingly gave up, and some things we were given no choice."

"Have I sacrificed something that I'm not aware of?"

"Your entire family has."

"What? Tell me. What have we given up?"

"Nathaniel is alive."

Paul's mouth dropped open. His head dropped back on the chair. All he could say was, "Alive? How?"

"After the incident with Priscilla, I made it my mission to find Nathaniel if he could be found. I put out feelers, and I eventually received some information. Nathaniel was being held at one of the worst facilities in the country. Without going into detail, many experiments are conducted there. It was imperative to formulate a plan quickly. Based on what Priscilla said about Nathaniel, I assumed he had a key, a way to escape. After much planning, we were able to get him out under cover of darkness. Nathaniel accepted the fact that he could not return home and put everyone in danger. Paul, he has been on the project from the time of his rescue."

"Why didn't you tell me?"

"What would you have done? I'll tell you what you would have done. You would have decided that your family would be better off with Nathaniel, and in so doing, you could have wrecked our mission. It was decided, with Nathaniel in complete agreement, that his whereabouts would remain a secret. Paul, he has been invaluable. His knowledge of plants and what they need comes so natural. He has a system on the vessel whereby we will grow most of our food while in flight. He has even calculated our needs for the first few years after we arrive. I know you would have liked to have known, but I just couldn't tell you. Please forgive me."

Paul sat stunned. His mind was swirling with thoughts of what might have been. "I'm sorry. What did you say?" His words would barely come out of his mouth.

"Paul, I need your forgiveness."

"Forgiveness?" Paul was drifting back to the matter at hand. "And for what is it that I'm forgiving you? Am I forgiving you for saving our only chance of escaping this reality? You were absolutely correct! I would have jeopardized the mission. I would have rationalized the situation and decided that we could have both, and if I had been wrong, well, we wouldn't be sitting here now would we?"

"No, I guess not," Reggie replied sheepishly.

"However, to knowingly deprive a child of his parent, now that's a different story. Reggie, I should be furious with you. From the time Pops was murdered and Dad disappeared, I had no male role model, but somehow I'm still here to talk about it. Nat has been lucky. He's had two grandfathers from whom to learn. I believe he'll be okay. So if it will relieve you of guilt, let me assure you that you are forgiven."

The ice in the room melted away. Reggie's normal skin color returned to his face as Paul continued, "However, forgiveness may not come as easily from Marsha."

Her name had no more left the tip of his tongue than Marsha came through the front door. "Reggie, when did you get here?"

"Just a while ago."

"Sorry to bother you fellows, but I need to get some scraps of fabric that I've been saving. Susie and I are just about ready to start a new quilt."

Paul rose to his feet. "Can you join us for a while?"

"You sound serious."

"I am."

"You're scaring me. Look, Reggie, Dad knows I have no intentions of leaving."

Reggie came to Paul's rescue. "Marsha, please sit. I have a note for you that will change things."

"Note? From whom? For what? Nothing is going to change." Marsha hesitatingly sat in the straight chair next to the fireplace.

Reggie reached inside his jacket and pulled out a small piece of paper. He gently placed the folded message in her hand and stepped back. He sensed she would need space when the words settled on her. She opened the fold. It read:

> Do as your dad says. Bring Mom and Dad with you.

A small heart was placed after the words.

"What's this about? Is this a cruel joke? Dad, surely you could have come up with something better than this."

All Paul could say was, "I haven't read the note. What does it say?"

Marsha all but threw the words at him. She was on her feet now, and she was pacing. Paul had never seen her this way. "Please, Marsha, settle down."

Marsha was passive, but eleven years of missing her husband had taken a toll. Now these two men were conning her into a situation that she had already refused. "Settle down? How could you?"

Reggie once again saved Paul. "Marsha, is that Nathaniel's handwriting?" Years had passed since she had read some of the old letters. She carefully retrieved the note. She opened the paper carefully. Tears filled her eyes. "Nathaniel said you would recognize his symbol." There it was. He ended everything he wrote to her with a heart but not just any heart. His hearts were curvy with a broken, wavy line through the middle. In very small letters, he always placed his initials on one side of the line and hers on the other side of the broken line. By now, she was sobbing. Paul held his daughter in his arms. They said nothing for a long while.

At last, the tears ceased. "Where is my husband?"

Reggie motioned to Paul to let him answer. He had been responsible for this secret, and it only seemed right that he should explain. "Do you remember the day of the abduction?"

"I can never forget."

"When the thugs left here, they took the men and Priscilla for processing."

"Processing?"

"Yes, they learned all they could about every aspect of their lives. The men were then shipped to different camps around the country. It took a long time, but I finally learned where Nathaniel had been sent. Marsha, it was a work farm. Believe it or not, much of the food that's available, which isn't much, comes from that place. With some inside help and our knowledge that Nathaniel had a key, we were able to penetrate the facility. It's a terrible place, Marsha. A person can be beaten for eating a morsel of the food that he has gathered. No mercy is shown. When the workers are all but dead from starvation, they conduct experiments on them. They say the tests are for the betterment of society. Marsha, it was a very dangerous endeavor, but we were able to get Nathaniel out late one night. We hid him for months. I suppose in a lot of ways we drilled him as well; however, ours was a friendly fact-finding effort. Once we knew enough, our mission was explained to him. Nathaniel and I were previously acquainted enough that he knew I could be trusted. We both realized he could never go home but that in time maybe home could come to him. Marsha, he kept up with you and Nat through the years. He even has a picture of you and Nat."

"How did he get it?"

Paul joined the conversation. "You're the one who took the photo out of my room. Pictures are so rare. Reggie, I was very upset over the lost picture, but I'm happy to know that it's in safe hands."

"Marsha, all I can say is I'm sorry. I'm sorry that I played a role in keeping your son and his father apart. I hope in time that you'll forgive me."

By this time, Marsha had somewhat settled her emotions. "I know I should be angry with you. I *am* angry, Reggie, but not at you. I'm furious over a society that will sit idly by and let these things happen. I'm mad that one small group of people can use another group like slaves. I'm indignant that I've been a part of the problem by not speaking at all. I've been submissive because I've always felt helpless." Marsha looked straight at Reggie. "Where is he?"

"He's at the launch site."

"Dad, my reason for not going has disappeared. I too have always wanted to be free of this bondage, but I never thought there was a sign of a chance. I want a better life for Nat. Dad, I'm ready whenever you are. I have several reasons to go now."

Reggie came right to the point. "I had planned to stay the night, but I think we should leave tonight instead. Your dad and I have a little business with the kinsmen. While we're gone, you go to Susie's house. Bring her, Ned, and Nat back here. Take nothing except the clothes on your back and enough food for two days. Water. Don't forget water as well."

"How much do I tell Ned and Susie?"

"Show them the note. Then explain that we're meeting Nathaniel. From there, we will be embarking on a freedom mission. Tell them the journey will be full of danger, but if we succeed, and we will, the cost will be well worth our efforts. Remember: take nothing but food, water, and the clothes on your back."

"What if they refuse to go?"

"The choice is theirs. Like everyone on this mission, they are free to go or stay behind."

Paul interrupted, "They'll go. They'll have no reason to stay here when you and Nat leave. Oh, they'll go all right. They've missed Nathaniel, too."

Marsha was much reassured with Paul's definite encouragement. Paul added, "Get back here as quickly as possible and wait on us. I'm not sure how long we'll be gone. We'll leave as soon as our meeting with the kinsmen is over."

"What's going on?" Confusion was in her voice.

"Oh, I just want to let the community know that we're leaving." Paul didn't dare tell her everything for fear the entire truth would cloud her optimism.

With those words, Paul grabbed his cane one last time, and he and Reggie headed for Zack Beard's home. He was the leader, and as such all business went through him. The leaders of the village came to be called kinsmen in the early years of the community when everyone was family. Through the years, the title "kinsman" had stuck with the group though many were no longer kin.

Paul and Reggie approached the Beard home. It looked like all the other homes in the village. As they climbed the porch steps, the door opened, and out popped Zack Beard. He was his usual jovial self. "What can I do for you two today?" Zack had met Reggie on an earlier visit, so introductions were unnecessary.

"I need to have a meeting with you and the kinsmen."

"Now, Gabe, if it's about yesterday's incident, we've already discussed the ramifications. Let me add we sure do appreciate what you did."

"You're welcome, Zack, but there's a little more to it than just what happened. We really need to address the entire group."

"Well, if you insist, I'll see what I can do. Go over to the school, and I'll see if I can round up the others. We'll meet you there."

Paul and Reggie backed down the steps and headed for the school. They both had a sense that Zack in no way understood the serious consequences of yesterday's visit. Upon arrival, the two men took a seat and waited for what seemed an eternity. Eventually the kinsmen filed in, each greeting the man they knew as Gabe Lawson. Paul introduced Reggie to the ones who had not met him. At last the meeting was brought to order by Zack. Zack made a few comments and then turned the floor over to Paul. Paul started, "You are all aware of yesterday's visit by the thugs. You are also aware of their belief that the village has smallpox. I fear very much that in time these people will return and do great harm to our village. We've all heard stories about entire villages being wiped out if those in control suspect an infectious disease. For this reason, I have two proposals to present to you. This village is small. There is another small community that has been abandoned. It is about twenty miles from here. The town could relocate without even being noticed if great care is imposed."

One of the kinsman spoke loudly, "I don't like that idea. What's the other choice?"

"My family and I will be leaving very soon. We can make arrangements for you all to go as well."

"Go where?" one of the men asked.

"I can't give you the details except to say that we'd be going far away."

"Is it dangerous?" another asked.

"Yes, but no more than staying here and watching the village burn."

Zack joined the fray, "Don't you think you're overstating the consequences of what happened yesterday. These people come from time to time, and then it will be years before we see them again."

Paul looked at Zack. It was like scales fell from his eyes, and he was seeing, really seeing Zack for the first time. This man had never had a family member abducted. He had never felt the pain that many of the others had experienced. He was the only person in the village who had the equipment to communicate with the outside world. Zack jolted Paul back. "I'm all for staying right here and doing nothing."

With Zack's leadership, the others one by one decided to do nothing. To ride out the crisis seemed to them to be the best approach. Paul saw no need to argue. Zack closed the meeting by telling Paul how much he and his family would be missed. Paul smiled and thanked the group for listening to his concerns. He and Reggie then left the building. Reggie then asked, "Why did you stop your argument?"

"It was going to do no good."

"How do you know that?"

"Didn't you notice how defensive Zack was. Zack has been the leader a long time. He fears change. Any move might mean a power shift. Zack doesn't want that. The community is small, but there are control issues even on this small scale. Zack doesn't have a desire for personal freedoms."

"What?"

"Yeah. Did you notice how he minimalized the brief argument that took place? He wasn't weighing the consequences of doing nothing. He's never lost a family member to the thugs. I question his judgment. Is there any reason we can't leave immediately?"

"None that I know of. I chose to leave a little later because there would be fewer chances of being noticed, but as far as I'm concerned, now is as good a time as any."

The two moved a little faster toward Paul's home. When they arrived, Ned, Susie, Marsha, and Nat were waiting on them. Ned said, "We're going, Gabe, I mean Paul. Marsha explained some things to us, but we have other questions."

"I know you do, and we'll try to answer them as best we can on our trip to meet Nathaniel. We had planned to leave later but have changed our minds. We're leaving now. Grab the supplies, and let's go."

All six headed for the utility vehicle. Paul fully expected the villagers to try to stop them, but nothing happened. Maybe Paul was growing paranoid. After loading, the vehicle made its way slowly down the gravel road. Reggie was driving. He said, "I need to tell you that this is no ordinary vehicle. That's why I'm travelling so slow. I don't want the holes and bumps to mess with the inner workings of this machine."

"What do you mean?" Paul asked.

"This vehicle was a product of late twentieth-century technology. People, we're armed. In the event anyone tries to bother us, we're prepared."

"What a waste," was all Paul could say.

"How so?"

"That a group of people was so smart yet they overlooked the preservation of their most important asset: freedom. It makes me sick to think of the waste."

That was all it took. When Nat heard the word *freedom*, he immediately wanted the answer to an all-important question that at once changed the mood of the group. "Do you think I might have a dog at this place we're going?" he asked.

The vehicle exploded with laughter. All the tension felt by the group melted away. Their very lives were on the line. Uncertainty loomed with every turn, and Nat was only interested in a dog. How typical of a child, and the adults loved it. Paul answered above the laughter, "I think we can arrange that. I understand some beautiful animals are making the trip."

Nat sat back in his seat. For the time being he was content in his world of planning for his special dog. But shortly the question came, "Reckon there's fishing holes where we're going?"

"Oh, I wouldn't be surprised if there's a Blubber out there waiting for us," Paul answered.

Up to this point, daydreaming had been useless. Now there was hope.

CHAPTER 17

The group traveled the rest of the day and night taking periodic breaks for food and rest. During one of those stops Reggie announced that he was pleased with their progress. "If we continue to make good time, we should arrive at the launch site about twilight."

"When do we plan to leave?" a cautious Marsha asked. Marsha had every reason to be cautious. She was still taking in the truth about the whereabouts of her husband. She feared she might barely see him and this life would suddenly end.

"As soon as we arrive and sanitize, the final stage of the countdown will begin. I'll be contacting the site when we are about thirty miles away so that everyone can make final preparations. Everything will happen very quickly, so I want you to be preparing yourself for the fast pace of those last minutes before lift off."

"Is there any special reason we are the last to arrive?"

"Oh, yes. Your dad is the only one on the planet who knows where we're going. We didn't want him at the site any earlier just in case something went wrong. He's just too valuable to take a chance on losing."

Marsha turned her attention to Paul. "And how long have you known of this place?"

"Since long before you were born."

The day wore on with the usual travel chitchat. The vehicle pulled over as Reggie announced one last break for the weary travelers. "We're about a hundred miles from the site. I'll be informing the others of our whereabouts in about an hour."

The six slowly emerged from the vehicle on a deserted stretch of road. Nat especially needed a break as he ran in circles around the parked vehicle. Everyone else stretched and walked to limber their bodies. For a moment, Reggie disappeared around the bend in the road ahead. Upon returning, Reggie motioned for the group to get into the vehicle. No one questioned him. After everyone was inside, he said, "I found a small detection device just ahead. I'm not sure why it would be here, but we're leaving the road and travelling around the instrument. The bad part is I don't know if we've gone through any others."

Just as the words left the cavern of his mouth, he spotted a vehicle quickly approaching them from the rear. "I guess it's too late to avoid anything now. We're staying on the road, and we're moving fast. Make sure you're buckled in real good."

All at once the vehicle made a hefty lurch forward. Ned quickly asked, "What was that?"

"I've put our invisible shields over the vehicle."

"You've done what?" Susie and Marsha asked at the same time.

"With these shields we should be protected against bullets."

"The vehicle looks like an ordinary utility vehicle to me," Susie added. She was soon to find out otherwise as the rather large truck approached the rear end of their vehicle.

It was obvious the truck meant to harm them. It was so close the group screamed. "I'm sure that thing hit us," Marsha screamed.

"Why didn't we feel anything?" Paul asked.

"It's part of the work of the shields." Reggie paused the conversation as he watched in the rear view mirror as the truck was preparing to ram once again. He also noticed a missile launcher was being prepared. "Everyone put your head down in your lap and hold on as tight as you can. I don't want to do this, but I see no other way." His hesitancy quickly turned to deadly action as he pressed the red button on the console. The utility vehicle did its best to turn into a projectile, but Reggie held it under control as the rear of the vehicle turned into a launching pad for two fiery missiles. The group heard a loud explosion, then quietness. Reggie halted the vehicle a safe distance from the inferno. He turned in his seat and watched the flames for a brief moment. He then announced, "These last hundred miles must be covered at top speed. I'm not sure what these people were up to, but it certainly wasn't good."

Paul glanced at Reggie and said, "You suppose Zack had something to do with this?"

"I don't suppose we'll ever find out, and you know, it doesn't really matter, now does it?"

Paul smiled rather weakly. "No, I don't suppose it does."

CHAPTER 18

The remainder of the trip was relatively trouble free. The high rate of speed at which they were travelling was the only significant problem. The ladies in the back became a little queasy but barely mentioned the problem for fear of causing a delay. At last the tall mountain that housed their home for the next two years was in front of them. Reggie breathed a sigh of relief and announced, "We're here."

Marsha exclaimed, "I don't understand."

With that, Reggie pointed at the side of the mountain, and the hidden hole appeared. The group collectively gasped. "They're expecting us, so once we're inside, we'll be sidestepping some of the usual security measures. We're the last ones in, so some of the usual precautions will be unnecessary."

For that reason, the group avoided the bone-chilling dark. The lights remained on, and they proceeded to the next room.

All Nat could say was, "Wow!" The others were speechless in awe of the technology.

Reggie at last spoke. "We'll be boarding a huge elevator next." The door opened to allow entry. The group was amazed at its size. Reggie continued as the machine moved upward, "When the door opens, you'll see your new home. We will not board until we've been sanitized and given our uniform. We will then enter the decompression area. After which, you will enter the main area and meet your shipmates. You will then be escorted to your living quarters. Twenty minutes before liftoff, you will return to the main area, where you will fasten yourself into a seat for the adventure of a lifetime."

As the huge room referred to as an elevator ascended, Paul thought, *There's no turning back now.* When the doors at last opened, a gasp rippled through the group. Never in their wildest dreams had the newcomers imagined such a machine existed. Marsha was near speechlessness but still managed to say, "I can't believe this."

"Oh, it's real, very real, and we're getting ready to leave here shortly aboard that machine," Reggie replied. "Now quickly move to the holding chamber to your left, where you will be sanitized."

They entered a rather large area. A door opened on the far end for the women to enter and disrobe. After which, sanitization sprinklers would gently spray the women, and they would be prepared to put their uniforms on and go through a sterile chute leading to the decompression area. Reggie pointed in the direction that he wanted Marsha and Susie to go. "Marsha, you and Susie will prepare in that room. Someone will be there to assist you. The rest of us will sanitize right here and join you in the decompression area."

Marsha and Susie obediently followed instructions. When they opened the door, a figure stood at the far end. Both women had assumed a lady would meet them, but as they approached the shape, it was apparent the greeter was a man. This was not just any man. They both froze. Marsha's arms dropped limply to her side. Susie jerked her hands over her mouth. Neither said anything. In fact, his name had barely been mentioned on the long trip to this place. It seemed to mention his name might suddenly make him go away. But there he was. Nathaniel *was* alive. Eleven years had been kind to the man. He was as handsome as ever. He too stopped in his tracks. He needed to look at the two women—one who gave him life, the other for whom he lived. Marsha was the first to speak. "Nathaniel?" she asked in disbelief. She ran in his direction, and he in hers. They wrapped their arms around each other. Marsha said through her tears, "I always knew you were alive. I never gave up. I didn't know how or when we'd reunite, but I always believed."

Marsha and Nathaniel were crying tears that had been held in for eleven years. Finally, Susie was allowed to join in the reunion. Tears flowed freely. They were tears of joy, tears for what might have been, and tears for lost moments.

When the three separated, they glanced at the open door. The boy stood silently with Reggie and his grandfathers as he watched the display. He was unsure whether he should join them; however, there was no question that this was the man of whom his mother had so often spoken. Nathaniel looked in the boy's direction. "Nat?"

"Dad?"

Nathaniel dropped to his knees as Nat ran to him. The two embraced in gratitude for the shared moment. They both sensed how much had been lost, but they also knew their circumstances were going to allow a future, hopefully a future filled with a genuine bond.

When the two released each other, Ned grabbed his son. It was a day Ned had never expected to see until a few days ago. Now everything had changed. A broken link in the family chain had been repaired. Life might be hard out there wherever they were going, but they would brave it together as a family.

Paul was the last to greet Nathaniel. Nathaniel looked straight into Paul's eyes. "Thank you for taking care of my family."

"Did you ever think otherwise?"

"Not for a moment."

"Nat has been under my influence for a long time. I hope he hasn't developed too many bad family traits." Paul laughed as he made the comment.

"I'm sure he's a fine young man."

"Oh, he is."

Reggie broke up the meeting. "Let's finish this cleaning process. Men, go to the outer room. Women, remain in this area." When the process was complete, the group made their way through a sterile chute into the decompression room. Reggie disconnected the chute. The only connection the vessel had to the earth at this point was the launch pad and the steel walkway leading directly from the decompression room to the elevator. "You are about to meet a few of your shipmates," Reggie said as he led them down the hallway that opened to the main area.

The group wanted to stop and look at the documents on the wall, but Reggie urged them on.

As they stepped through the door, they were greeted with applause. Most knew the story of Nathaniel and Marsha and were very happy for them. Others knew Paul held the map for their destination. Numerous introductions were made. As Paul was about to be introduced to one of the men who was very close to the same age as himself, he stopped the person, "No introduction is necessary."

The two men looked intently at each other. "Indeed there is no need," the other responded.

"How have you been, Carney?"

"The same as yourself."

"Can you believe after all these years our paths would cross in this way?"

The two remained silent for a while. Each was thinking about the many days they had spent together at the state school, of how they shared written secrets and then destroyed the notes. "Things are going to be different now, Paul. We have something now that we didn't have back then."

"What's that?"

"Hope, Paul. We have hope."

The two smiled, and their years and years of separation melted away. "Carney, you do know that things you taught me enabled me to find this place, don't you?"

"When I was brought in, your name came up. I strongly suspected you had used some of the things I showed you. You did erase all knowledge of this place, didn't you?"

"Gone forever."

Reggie joined Paul and Carney. "I hate to break up the party, but it's time to begin the countdown."

Paul and Carney stood still as everyone else made their way to the seating area. "Come on, Gramps. Come with us," Nat said.

"I'll see you after the launch when we're able to move around," Paul told the boy. Paul could only hope and pray that the liftoff wouldn't be a fatal disaster. He took a long look at Nat. He tried to memorize every cell of his face. He didn't want this to be the last time he ever saw him, but the possibility existed.

Nat grabbed Paul. "I love you, Gramps."

"I love you more than life, Nat."

Nat waved at Paul as he left the area. Reggie motioned for Paul and Carney to follow him. They strode down several hallways and finally entered the command post. This area was humming with activity. There were three empty seats beckoning to the men. "Here's where we'll be stationed through takeoff, and where we'll work throughout the trip. Paul, it's time to lock in the coordinates. Are you ready? Once they're punched in and locked, there's no reversing them until we're out of the gravitational pull of the earth."

The room became silent. "Now seems like a splendid time," Paul said. Paul asked the ladies in the room to glance away as he dropped his pants to below his hips. There those precious numbers were tattooed in a straight line from his hipbone to his navel.

"This is what you meant when you said, 'They're always with me!' I thought you had them memorized."

"Oh, I do, but that was a little risky."

Paul read the coordinates to the chief navigator. He punched them in and paused. Looking directly at Paul, he said, "Impossible. There's nothing there."

There were gasps throughout the area. "Oh, I assure you it's there."

"Where? No such place is being located."

While all the questions were being asked, Carney was busy on the machine in front of him. He was pecking keys as fast as they'd permit. "Wrong. It's there. Take a look."

The navigator along with the captain quickly made their way to Carney's machine. There it was exactly where Paul had said it was. Paul leaned over and whispered to Carney, "I thought I erased it forever."

"Oh you did, and you hid it quite well from everyone but me." He smiled and walked over to the others leaving Paul to wonder how he located the planet.

The captain asked, "Is everyone ready? All the passengers are buckled into their seats. When the lock button is pressed, liftoff will occur in twenty minutes."

"Just a moment," Paul spoke. "Just as the early settlers prayed for divine guidance, I think we should as well."

One by one everyone in the control room dropped to his knees. When the room was completely silent, the captain's voice carried a prayer for guidance, direction, and thanks. "Dear God, we ask that you guide us on this perilous journey. We don't know what to expect, but we're willing to be used for the cause of freedom. Please bless our path and keep us safe. We ask these things in the name of Jesus. Amen." When he finished, the group echoed his final amen.

They were now ready to engage the lock button. With solemn fingers, the captain pressed the bright red button.

He looked around the room and said, "It's done." A hush filled the room as he announced to his passengers that the final countdown had begun. The travelers were told they would get a five-minute warning at the end of which liftoff would occur.

At fifteen minutes and counting, the captain said, "No, I don't believe this."

Reggie jumped to attention. "What's wrong?"

"Look."

Reggie looked at the screen that transmitted images from the outside. "No! How far away are they?"

"Maybe five miles."

"Can we detonate the explosives?"

"That can only be done from the wall just inside the dark area. That's not the worst of it."

Reggie looked again and grimaced as he realized they were carrying missiles. "Can they blow us out of the air?"

"If we don't stop them, that's exactly what they'll do."

"Do I have enough time to get to the dark room and back?"

"It's a long shot."

Paul was listening intently. "Reggie, I'll go. I'm old, and I've contributed my part to the mission. Your job is just beginning." Paul unbuckled his harness and said, "Quick, tell me where to go and what to do!"

Reggie didn't want Paul to go, but there was no time for an argument. The lift-off time was locked, and it could not be stopped. Their fate was sealed. The clock was ticking. Reggie and Paul were running down the hall. Reggie was giving instructions as they moved as fast as they could. "Just as you enter the dark area, you'll see a bright red light to your right. It's enclosed in glass. A hammer hangs below it. Grab the hammer, break the glass, and press the button four times. This will activate all four charges when the trucks cross the cameras' eyes. Then get back up here as fast as lightning. I'm opening all hatches and locking them open. You won't have to wait on anything. Be sure to lock the elevator door open when you exit." Reggie was out of breath by the time they reached the decompression area. "Paul, this door will start to close at thirty seconds until liftoff. It can't be opened again until we are well on our way. Hurry! Go! Godspeed!"

Paul ran across the metal bridge. No one would have ever guessed he was seventy-five years old. He was in the run of his life. The elevator door was open. He pressed the ground button. Time stood still, though in reality seconds were quickly passing. He tried to will the elevator to move faster to no avail. Finally the door opened. He locked the elevator open and ran through the long corridors as fast as he could. Time was not on his side. He didn't know how much time had passed, but he knew it was in short supply. At last, he arrived at the dark room. He immediately saw the red light. Strange, how the darkness of his earlier visits had always blocked the glowing light. Somehow the room did not seem as ominous as it had on his other visits. He grabbed the hammer and broke the glass. He pressed the red button four times and prayed, "Give me strength and time to get back to the ship." Paul ran like the wind. The corridors seemed to extend forever. He didn't even realize that he was as physically able as he was. He jumped on the elevator, unlocked the door, and pushed the top button. The elevator appeared to barely move. *Kaboom*. The entire elevator swayed as all four charges exploded one after the other. No matter whether he made it or not, he had ensured the safe departure of the ship.

At last the door opened just as the computer-generated voice announced, "Twenty-five seconds and counting."

Paul could see through the thick smoke that the door was starting to close, and he still had to cross the metal bridge. He was determined to make it. He willed his body one last effort to beat the quickly closing door. The opening had closed to below waist high on him. He didn't want to do it, but he hit the deck shoulder first and rolled inside the decompression area. There was no time to do anything but grab the metal supports of the benches on the wall. He heard the engines roar. It was deafening. Then the movement came. They were actually moving upward. Then the pain came. He felt his face grow tense. It was becoming harder and harder to breathe. He needed relief. Paul tightly closed his eyes to avoid seeing what might come next. Then all was quiet.

CHAPTER 19

Paul heard a sound in the far distance. At first he was unsure if his hearing was deceiving him, but there it was again. He opened his eyes, and there she was. She was running full speed, and he could tell she was happy. It had been a lifetime ago, but the Beast remembered him. Her tongue lolled to the side as she drooled for joy. In another life, Paul would have attempted to divert the wetness, but he was so happy to see her that he didn't mind the slobber. There she was jumping into the same position that she was in the last time he had seen her alive. There were no grudges. The Beast felt no great compulsion to forgive him. Forgive him for what? Forgive him for being a little boy who was not wise to the evil in the world? No, the Beast loved Paul then, and she loved him even more now. "Where am I, girl?" Paul asked as if expecting an answer. He looked around, and he knew. "My goodness, I'm home."

Paul found himself walking down the long drive that led straight to G's house. The Bradford pears were in full bloom, and the blossoms were falling gently all over him. With each step, he felt like he was in a ticker-tape parade. He stooped to examine one of the silky petals. The tiny blossom was gold tipped. Never had he seen anything like it. He eased the petal into his pocket just as he realized all the blossoms were gold tipped. The white, four-board plank fence that surrounded the beautiful farm was just as he remembered except… the fence wasn't made of wood. Paul stepped off the drive and moved toward the fence. He ran his hand across the top board. It was smooth and shimmery, almost like glass. Upon closer inspection, he discovered the fence was made of a continuous pearl. The shimmer was produced by tiny diamonds that were ingrained inside the pearl. For a moment, Paul lost himself as he studied the fence. It was absolutely amazing. He looked out over the farm and sensed the entire plot held special surprises but perhaps none more inviting than the scent that was floating on the air. Just as he had recognized the sound of the Beast, the smell was so familiar. It beckoned him toward the house.

As Paul and the Beast approached the huge house, it too was as he remembered except it sparkled. Whereas the fence had tiny diamonds in the pearl, the house had large diamonds within a heavy pearl exterior that was supported by a solid diamond foundation. Paul thought how like Pops it was to have the outside so well coordinated.

Paul heard movement in the house, and out of nowhere stepped G with a plate of chocolate chip bars. She stopped in her tracks. "I received word a while ago to expect a guest. I strongly suspected it would be you," she said with a sad joy. She laid the delectables on a table and held out her arms to Paul. “Come here, baby, and give me a big hug.”

Paul couldn’t get to her fast enough. It had been so long since he had seen the strong-willed woman. Somehow she seemed more at peace than he could ever recall. The two embraced for a long while. She then pulled free. “Let me take a long look at you. You’re all grown up.”

“I’m more than grown up, G. I’m seventy-five years old.”

“Oh, I know, but you’ll always be my little angel.”

Paul was anxious. “Is Pops around?”

“Oh, yes. Didn’t you see the tractors as you came up the drive? No, I guess you didn’t. He’s plowing the back side of the farm today.”

“You said tractors. Who else is plowing?”

“Oh, it’s just a young man that came to us a long time ago.”

Paul was so taken by all the sights that he didn’t even ask the person’s name. Instead, he asked, “What are they growing?”

“You get one guess.”

“It must be corn.”

“Nope. Flowers. Pops grows the most gorgeous flowers in the kingdom. It’s his job to furnish the beautiful plants for all the special gatherings. See those salvia next to the fountain?” Paul glanced in the direction of one of Pops’s flowerbeds. “Take a close look.”

Paul walked over to the flowers. “G, these red salvia have rubies growing on them. The purple ones have amethysts. I’ve never seen anything like them.”

"The Master didn't mean for you to see anything like this before arriving. Take a close look at the foliage."

"Wow! The leaves are coated with emeralds. How is this possible?"

"All things are possible here."

"G, it's so wonderful to be home."

Paul grabbed a cookie bar and ate three before sitting down in the most comfortable wicker rocker he had ever sat in. He noticed G was staring intently toward the drive, but he supposed her to be thinking. "You're not staying." Her words caught him off guard.

"What?"

"It's not your time. You've got to go back."

"No! I won't!"

She slowly turned and faced him. "From time to time, we're allowed to catch a glimpse of the happenings from the other side." She paused to let the words settle. "Paul, I'm so proud of you. You didn't squander your chance at obtaining freedom. You recognized that one chance, and you grabbed it. You have lived most of your life seeking the opportunity to be free, and you will know the joy that only freedom can bring."

"But I'm free here. I've never felt more free." Paul was starting to become quite agitated.

"I know, baby, but your work is not finished."

"It could be."

"Sugar plum, I know you think you've completed your part of the mission, but you haven't."

"What else could I possibly do?"

"You offer hope." She paused once again. "We don't usually tell our visitors about the future, but occasionally we have special permission to speak. This is one of those times. Paul, your journey will be a success but not without trials. Those brave souls aboard that vessel are going to need to hear from you. Paul, you're one of the few left who has experienced a free life. They're going to need to know that everything will be fine. Tell me you'll willingly go back."

Paul got the distinct impression that he was going to be going back whether he wanted to or not.

"Baby, it won't be long before you'll be right back here. Next time, you'll be staying."

The far-off roar of the tractor stopped. G appeared to be getting nervous. "It's time to go."

"Can't I stay a little longer?"

It pained G to refuse his request, but she had to send him away quickly. She knew if Pops and the others gathered as she expected they would, he might never leave. "Paul, I want you to walk down that driveway just like you walked in here. Do not turn around." She grabbed him one last time and kissed his cheek so hard his head moved. "I'll make sure the Beast stays with me. I love you, darling."

"I love you more, G."

Paul slowly trudged toward the driveway. His heart was heavy. He wanted so badly to stay. He knew G had her reasons, and he would have to trust her. Paul heard talking on the porch, and it was more than one person. "Keep walking, baby. Don't look back."

If Paul had turned around at that moment, there was no way he could or would have returned to the other side. For there gathered on that porch were family members from Paul's past. There stood G and Pops and Mom and Dad and Renee and a nameless young man who bore a striking resemblance to Paul with the gentle eyes of Renee. He was a man who should have had a full life on the other side, but whose existence was stolen.Paul was almost to the end of the drive when he heard a voice so familiar to him.

"Paul!"

He stopped, but it was too late.

CHAPTER 20

"Dad! Please wake up!" Paul opened his eyes to an almost hysterical Marsha. He was lying in the hospital ward aboard the vessel. Marsha was shaking him.

"Where am I?" Paul asked.

The doctor jumped. He was visibly rattled by the voice. "You're in the sick ward."

"What happened?"

"Let's just say that you're alive, and that's a miracle."

Paul turned toward Marsha. "Tell me what happened. I remember diving for the half-open latch. I rolled under one of the benches and held on. I remember going up and the pain that followed. I must have blacked out."

Marsha couldn't believe her eyes. Her dad was actually alive. Her mourning quickly turned to joy as she answered him, "Oh, it was a bit more than that. After we were safely on our way, we were told by the captain that we could safely maneuver the ship. I glanced up, and

Reggie and Carney were dashing like wild men toward the decompression area. I thought it a bit strange that you were not with them. The next thing I knew Reggie was going toward the sick ward with you in his arms and Carney in tow. I don't know how he managed to carry you, but he did. I immediately followed. They handed you off to the doctors, who immediately started to work on you. Dad, they pronounced you dead not more than a minute ago."

"I was," Paul said softly.

"Oh Dad," Marsha replied mournfully.

"It's okay. I'm back, and I'm with my family. Is Nat okay?"

"Yes, he's fine. He handled liftoff like a real trooper."

"Where are Reggie and Carney?"

"They're outside. As you might imagine, they're quite upset." Marsha smiled and moved toward the door. "I'll break the news and bring them in."

Marsha gently closed the door behind her. She moved in the direction of the two troubled men and broke into a smile. "He didn't leave us, at least not for good."

"What!" they both exclaimed and jumped to their feet. "He's alive?"

"He sure is. He's talking. It's as if nothing happened. I believe he's going to be just fine."

"Let's go in!" Reggie said, looking at Carney and Marsha.

The three entered the room very quietly. They were still unsure whether to believe his existence. Maybe Marsha was mistaken. Perhaps she wanted him to live so badly she'd hallucinated to the point she actually believed he spoke. They moved to Paul's bedside. Paul opened his eyes. He really was living and breathing. Reggie spoke first. "You really gave us a scare."

"You were scared? What about me as I made that shoulder roll at the last possible moment." Paul smiled. "We're on our way, aren't we?"

"You better believe it," Carney said.

Reggie looked at Paul solemnly. "If you hadn't been willing to go outside, we wouldn't have made it past the liftoff. Paul, they would have blown us out of the sky. Instead, we're well on our way. All the readings are good, and all the travelers are safe. We can never show our appreciation enough."

"Oh yes we can," Carney said.

"How?" Reggie asked.

"Let's make the journey a success."

"Oh, we'll do that," Reggie replied.

"I can say with a certain degree of certainty that we're going to be very successful," Paul said. Paul smiled as he thought of G's prediction. His journey to the other side gave him a renewed strength, a determination. He would never be the same. He would be different, but it would be a good difference.

Reggie and Carney said their good-byes and quietly left the room. When they opened the door, the hallway was full of travelers. "Is he going to be okay?" they asked.

"Oh yes. He's going to be just fine."

A cheer went up that penetrated the door that separated them from their hero.

Paul heard the noise. "What's that about?"

"It's for you, Dad. Just close your eyes and enjoy the moment."

"I will in a minute, but first, I have something for you."

"What do you have for me?"

Paul reached into his pocket. "Close your eyes and hold out your hand."

"Is this going to scare me?"

"Of course not. Just do as I say."

She closed her eyes tight and held out her hand. When she opened her eyes, the most beautiful blossom she had ever seen lay in the palm of her hand. She looked at it in amazement. "This is beautiful. No, it's more than beautiful. It's the most gorgeous petal I've ever seen. Is that gold on the edge?"

"Oh, yes."

"Where did you get this?"

"Let's just say it came from a faraway place."

Marsha looked at her dad. It was a look that said she knew where the gift originated. She would ask questions later. For now, Paul rested. He was content. Paul Allen was a free man, and that's the way God intended it to be. *Free.* What a beautiful word. What a wonderful word indeed.

EPILOGUE

The sun rose bright and cheerful the following morning. All citizens were expected to watch the state-sponsored news report each morning. The elites deemed it important to be informed citizens. As members of various communities gathered around the state broadcast boxes, a lovely face appeared. There was no chitchat. She went straight to her purpose. Her stories included many of the social happenings of the elites. She reported parties that the powerful elites had given and the names of those in attendance. Finally, on a more serious note, she reported that a small village in the hill country had an outbreak of smallpox. The state had sent armed healthcare workers into the village. The workers saw no way to help its occupants and ordered the village burned to prevent the spread of the disease. The fate of the villagers was unknown.

The anchor didn't so much as pause as she continued the state's version of the news. Her next story involved the explosions that had occurred in the desert the night before. Nearby towns had buildings that were damaged from the loud booms. Scientists believed a huge meteorite had crashed into the earth. As the story was reported, a video, which some unknown person had filmed, was shown that caught the action from a distance. At the close of the story, not one soul questioned that the booms occurred before the streak across the sky, and no one noticed that the meteorite was going up, not down. When the last word of the story was spoken, the screen went blank.